He spoke quietly, without looking at her.

"There were times when my rage, my determination to find you and get even with you, was the only thing that sustained me."

She smiled a sad little smile. "I swore never to speak to you again. I vowed to myself never to need you again. Never to ask anything of you."

When she didn't go on, he prompted, "And now?"

"I realize you'll never look at me and see something other than a collaborator with your enemies."

He peered at her in the dusk, trying to make out the expression in her eyes. But she'd averted her face until all he saw was a glistening track down her cheek.

After a moment, she continued. "If there's anything I can do to help you catch the people who kidnapped you, I'll do it. Just say the word."

He turned over her words for a while. Finally he said gravely, "I do have one request of you."

"Name it."

"Kiss me."

The Soldier's Secret Daughter

CINDY DEES

MILLS & BOON®

First published in Great Britain 2012
by Mills & Boon, an imprint of Harlequin (UK) Limited.
Large Print edition 2012
Harlequin (UK) Limited,
Eton House, 18-24 Paradise Road,
Richmond, Surrey TW9 1SR

© Cynthia Dees 2009

ISBN: 978 0 263 22991 2

Harlequin (UK) policy is to use papers that are natural, renewable and recyclable products and made from wood grown in sustainable forests. The logging and manufacturing process conform to the legal environmental regulations of the country of origin.

Printed and bound in Great Britain
by CPI Antony Rowe, Chippenham, Wiltshire

CINDY DEES

started flying airplanes while sitting in her dad's lap at the age of three and got a pilot's license before she got a driver's license. At age fifteen, she dropped out of high school and left the horse farm in Michigan where she grew up to attend the University of Michigan.

After earning a degree in Russian and East European Studies, she joined the U.S. Air Force and became the youngest female pilot in the history of the Air Force. She flew supersonic jets, VIP airlift, and the C-5 Galaxy, the world's largest aeroplane. She also worked part-time gathering intelligence. During her military career, she travelled to forty countries on five continents, was detained by the KGB and East German secret police, got shot at, flew in the first Gulf War, met her husband and amassed a lifetime's worth of war stories.

Her hobbies include professional Middle Eastern dancing, Japanese gardening and medieval reenacting. She started writing on a one dollar bet with her mother and was thrilled to win that bet with the publication of her first book in 2001. She loves to hear from readers and can be

My warmest thanks to Carla Cassidy and Marie Ferrarella for their inspiration and support with this series. You two wear some pretty classy coattails—thanks for letting me hitch a ride on them!

Chapter 1

Jagger Holtz crouched in the dark as the helicopter overhead peeled away, ostensibly to continue tracking traffic jams on the highways below. They'd hovered over the AbaCo building a total of twenty-eight seconds. Just long enough to drop him on a zip line to the roof of the twenty-story-tall glass-and-steel tower. And hopefully not long enough to trigger the intense security of AbaCo Inc., one of the largest—and most shadowy—shipping firms in the world.

Bent over at the waist, he ran for cover, ducking behind a giant air-conditioning vent and taking a quick time check. He'd give AbaCo's goons three minutes to respond. Then, barring any company on the roof, he'd move on to phase two: infiltrating the building proper. He didn't expect to find his missing colleagues tonight—Hanson and MacGillicutty were fellow government agents sent into AbaCo undercover months ago. And both of them had disappeared. No messages. No distress signals. No evidence of foul play. They were just...gone. When his superiors had approached him, he'd leaped at the chance to do this risky mission.

It was starting to look as though his rooftop landing had gone unnoticed. He tied off a rope to a sturdy steel grille and checked his rappelling harness one more time. Down the side of the building, in through an office window and then they'd see if the password they'd bought from the snitch worked.

Without warning, all hell broke loose. The heavy steel doors on each of the four stairwells leading to the roof burst open with a deafening crash. Armed men rushed out, sweeping the roof with automatic weapons. They sprinted forward, quartering the roof with brutal efficiency.

Holy crap. Commandos for a helicopter overhead for twenty-eight seconds?

He slammed to the ground just as a high-intensity flashlight beam passed over his position, barely missing lighting him up like a Christmas tree. He was trapped. He gripped the metal grille in front of his face in frustration as they closed in on him. Warm, moist air blew at him like an incongruous sea breeze on this frigid Denver night.

Air. An air vent. It might be a dead end, but it was better than lying here and getting captured or killed in the next few seconds. He grabbed his pocketknife and used the blade to unscrew the nearest fastener holding the vent shut. He lobbed the thumb-sized screw as hard as he could across the roof. It clattered loudly, and shouting and a scramble of men reacted instantly.

The second screw popped loose. It went flying in another direction.

C'mon, c'mon. The last screw finally popped free. He grabbed the bottom of the grille and yanked. Someone was shouting irritably at the guards in German to quit running around like chickens, to form up and to search the roof methodically. Not good. AbaCo's serious security team was up here if they were speaking German.

Working fast, he slapped the clip from the rope he'd already tied off onto his climbing harness and rolled over the edge. He fell into space, fetching up hard as the rope caught. He bit back a gasp of pain as his groin took a hit from the harness that all but permanently unmanned him. Oww. So much for the glory of being a special agent.

The vent was about six by six feet square. Twisting until his feet braced against the side, he walked backward down the galvanized aluminum wall, doing his damnedest to be as silent as possible. The echo of any noise in here would be magnified a dozen times.

How far down the black shaft he descended, blind and lost, he had no idea. He counted steps and tried to estimate how far he'd gone. But it was hard to focus with periodic bursts of air from below knocking him off the wall and sending him spinning wildly in space, hanging on for dear life at the end of his single, skinny rope.

Hopefully, the AbaCo powers that be would declare the whole thing a false alarm and satisfy themselves with complaining to the radio station about its helicopter parking in their airspace. Otherwise, guards were probably waiting for him at the other end of this shaft, licking their chops at the prospect of nabbing themselves a third hapless federal agent. The idea of failing galled him, not only because he never failed, but also because it would mean Hanson and MacGillicutty were no closer to being found, their families no closer to any answers. Both of them had wives. Kids. Christmas last week had been hard on them all.

He guessed he was about halfway to the ground floor when the main shaft narrowed enough that he was forced to stop using his feet. He lowered himself hand over hand down the rope until his arms went so numb he could no longer feel them. His watch said the descent took twenty-four minutes. It felt like twenty-four hours.

Plenty of time to ponder the symbolism of his descent. Into darkness and silence and utter isolation. The hell he so richly deserved. He pushed away the encroaching panic. He could *not* afford to lose it now. He was a long way from out of this mess.

The air rushing up at him began to smell of car exhaust. The underground parking garage, maybe? Hmm. It had possibilities. Light began to glow faintly from below. Between his feet, he made out what looked like a metal grille. It was a miniature version of the big one on the roof.

The screws holding it in place were unfortunately on the other side, out of reach. He paused, listening carefully for any sound of humans nearby. Nothing. He damn well didn't intend to climb all the way back up that rope, some twenty stories. He slammed both feet into the metal panel, jumping on it with his full body weight. The slats bent slightly. He jumped again. And again. After a few more tries, a tiny gap showed at the edge of the grille as the metal began to buckle. He kicked again.

Crud. It sounded like Godzilla tearing a car apart with his teeth. Metal screeched, protesting harshly. This had to be drawing the entire cavalry to the garage. His only hope was to break through fast and get away from here before they arrived.

The grille's fasteners gave way all at once. He tumbled to the floor below, landing hard on the concrete. He grunted and rolled fast toward the nearest large object, a sedan parked on the slanting ramp, pulling his sidearm as he went. He scrambled under the car, then paused, scanning the area carefully for any feet. The goons weren't here yet.

He froze as a car drove past his position, winding its way out of sight into the bowels of the parking garage. Hurrying, he unzipped his backpack and pulled out a dark gray tweed suit coat before he stuffed the pack behind a concrete pillar. He donned the jacket over his black turtleneck and black slacks. A quick tug into place, and he was instantly transformed from commando to party crasher.

Now to find a patsy. A single female to walk him past the inevitable security. He glanced around at the cars. Mostly modest domestic cars and the occasional junker. Perfect. The worker bees' parking level.

The party was scheduled to start at eight o'clock. His watch said it was 8:05 p.m. The guests should be arriving in quantity right about now. He stood in a shadow near the elevator and settled in to wait. He pulled out a pack of cigarettes in case he needed a quick excuse to be loitering here. He didn't smoke, but the many other handy uses of cigarettes—including convenient cover story—made them a staple in his arsenal of secret-agent equipment.

In a few minutes, he spotted a vaguely human shape coming down the ramp toward him. Pink parka. Scarf wrapped around the face. Mittens. Ski hat under the parka hood. Fleece-lined suede boots. The apparition looked like a four-year-old kid bundled up by Mom to go out in the first big snow of the year to play. But more importantly, the apparition was alone.

Bingo. He had target acquisition. Or at least a way into the party.

Emily Grainger looked up, alarmed, as a tall man stepped out of the shadows next to the elevator. He stopped beside her, staring at the elevator door for a moment before surprising her by speaking. Men didn't usually speak to her. "Cold night, eh?"

She had to turn her whole upper body to see him out of her deep hood, and she did so awkwardly. She caught her first good look at him and started. Men like him definitely didn't speak to her. "Oh!" she exclaimed softly. "Uh, yes. I guess it is. Cold, that is."

She looked away, embarrassed at the way she was staring. He wasn't so much handsome as he was intense. His cheeks were deeply carved, his skin tanned as though he spent most of his time outdoors. His eyes were pale blue, nearly colorless, and as intense as the rest of him. His mouth was a little bit too wide, his nose a little too big. But still, it was a face a person would struggle to look away from. The man looking out through those intelligent, all-too-observant eyes was captivating.

He looked ready to explode into motion at the slightest provocation, just like…just like James Bond. He gave off that same restless, devil-may-care charm guaranteed to sweep a girl right off her feet. And he'd just said hello to her! Well, then.

She stared straight ahead at the stainless-steel elevator door. It threw back at her a blurry reflection of a pink whale.

Her entire life, she'd dreamed of meeting a man like this. Of becoming a different kind of woman—adventurous, bold and sexy—the kind of woman a man like this would fall for. And here he was. Her dream man in the flesh. She wasn't fool enough to believe a man like this would come along twice in her lifetime. This was it. Now or never.

"I don't think we've met before," he murmured. "What department do you work in?"

"Uh, I'm in accounting," she managed to

mumble in spite of her sudden inability to draw a complete breath. The elevator dinged and the steel panel started to slide open.

"Accounting. That's interesting."

Liar. Accounting wasn't interesting at all. It was boring. Safe and predictable and orderly. She couldn't count how often she wanted to jump up from her desk in her neat, bland little cubicle and scream. What she wouldn't give to be a sexy international spy like James Bond courteously holding the elevator door open for her now.

Her imagination took off. He had no idea who she was. She could be that other woman with him tonight. Flirtatious. Aggressive. The kind of woman who went after men like him and seduced them with a snap of her fingers. She envisioned ritzy casinos, champagne flutes and diamonds. Lots of flashy diamonds.

"What's your name?" James Bond murmured.

"Uh, Emily. Emily Grainger." Lord. Even her name sounded boring and safe. And it was too late to lie and call herself something exotic and alluring.

He smiled at her.

Stunned, she turned to face the elevator's front and about fell over her own feet. Ho. Lee. Cow. He had the greatest smile she'd *ever* seen. It was intimate and sexy and dangerous—all the things she imagined Bond's smile would be and more. It drew her in. Made her part of his secret double life. Promised things that no nice girl dared to think of.

"I'm Jagger," he murmured. "Jagger Holtz."

The name startled her. He didn't look like one of the Germans of the heavy contingent of them within AbaCo. And yet she probably shouldn't have been surprised. He had that same leashed energy, the same self-contained confidence that all the German security types within the firm had. But the way he'd pronounced it had been strange. Her understanding of the German language was that *J*s were pronounced like Americans pronounced a *Y*. So shouldn't his name have been Yagger? Why would he Americanize the name when none of the other Germans in the company bothered to do so?

She turned her whole upper body to look at him again. "What nationality is that name?"

He grinned self-deprecatingly, a lopsided, boyish thing that charmed the socks right off her. "I'd like to say it's a German name, but the truth is my mother was a Rolling Stones groupie. I think I'm actually named after Mick Jagger."

Her laughter startled her. A girl wasn't supposed to laugh at James Bond, was she?

The door opened, and she jumped when he reached out to steady her elbow. "Watch your step," he murmured.

Electricity shot down, or rather up, her arm, skittered across the back of her neck and exploded low in her belly. Whoa. Did James Bond have this effect on all the girls? No wonder he landed whoever he set his cap for! One touch from him and the women were putty in his hands!

Breathe, Emily. Breathe. Or more accurately, stop hyperventilating, Emily.

How she made it out of the elevator without falling over her feet, she had no idea. Her lower body had come completely unhinged from her central nervous system thanks to that devastating touch on her elbow. Not to mention that clutzy was her middle name. Particularly when she was flustered. And Jagger Holtz definitely flustered her.

"Maybe you'd better just take my arm," he said.

Good call. Give James credit for knowing a damsel in distress when he saw one. Or maybe he just knew he had that effect on all women.

She'd have been embarrassed, except he offered her his forearm with such obvious pleasure at the prospect of her touching him that she was more stunned than anything else. Was he blind? Or so hopelessly nearsighted he didn't realize how plain she was? How...completely average?

Of course, he hadn't actually seen much of her, truth be told. She was wrapped up like a mummy and only her eyes and the tip of her nose were visible. She sighed. He'd figure out soon enough that she was a mousy little thing and not even close to flashy enough to be seen with him. He was the sort of man who would look at home with a supermodel on his arm. The fantasy had been fun while it lasted, at any rate.

They stepped into the lobby of the AbaCo building. The soaring atrium, nearly eight stories tall, was decorated from top to bottom with metallic silver Christmas decorations. Personally, she didn't like them. They seemed too cold and impersonal. Hard, even. But then, that wasn't a bad approximation of the personality of her employer, she supposed.

The shipping firm was intensely German, although it had offices in a dozen major cities around the world. But AbaCo took its Teutonic persona very seriously. There were rules for everything, the rules got followed and the cargo got where it was going on time. Or else heads rolled.

"Can I hang up your coat for you?" Jagger asked pleasantly.

She looked up from bending over awkwardly as she tried to pry off one of her boots. She'd brought a pair of shoes to change into for the party, in her bulky purse. "Uh. Wow. That's really polite of you. I guess so."

She postponed her boots and straightened. He was behind her immediately, slipping her parka off her shoulders as gracefully as if it were a mink coat.

"Nice dress," he murmured on cue.

Man. He didn't miss a trick. He'd clearly aced Date Etiquette 101. Whoa. Back up. Date? They'd met in the parking garage and ridden up in the elevator together. She'd indulged in a momentary fantasy, and that was about as close to a date as they were ever going to get. He was already striding away from her, in fact.

Although in defense of her fantasy, he was carrying her coat to the cloakroom for her. Presumably, he would return with a ticket for her to pick it up later. So he would have to speak with her at least one more time tonight. One more moment to indulge in the idea of a "them." Her and James Bond. She smiled blissfully. In her world, these little fantasies were about as close as she ever got to the real thing, so why not enjoy them?

If only she had the guts to turn her day-dreams into reality.

One thing AbaCo did very well was throw a party. Caterers had set up a buffet line at the far end of the atrium, and she knew from previous New Year's Eve parties that the food would be delicious. A band was playing background music at the moment but would shift into dance music as midnight approached. And then there was the open bar, of course. Bartenders ranged behind it, ready and waiting to serve nearly a thousand employees and their guests at this, the North American headquarters for the company.

Jagger was back almost before she'd had time to slip into the daring pair of red stilettos she'd given herself for Christmas. She would never dream of wearing them to work, but she hadn't been able to resist them when she'd seen them. They reminded her of Dorothy's shoes from *The Wizard of Oz,* but naughtier, with their open toes and sling backs. She was suddenly fiercely glad she'd splurged on them as Jagger strode back toward her. Her hands went to her hair nervously, smoothing the static electricity from her hat out of its silky brunette length.

His mouth quirked into a smile as if he enjoyed her sudden self-consciousness. Laughter jumped into her eyes in response. After all, it really was a very good joke to think that he might actually find her attractive.

His gaze rather improbably slid lower as he moved toward her. Right. As if there was anything to look at in her drab body. She supposed she was reasonably proportioned, but she was no supermodel. She actually had breasts and hips, and her legs, although shapely, weren't a mile long. She barely topped five foot four.

Even more improbably, a slow grin spread across Jagger's face as he took in the view, from her slinky red dress all the way down to her sexy shoes and back up again. *Oh. My. Goodness.*

He must be drunk. He was acting as though he actually found her attractive.

He held both hands out to her as he reached her, taking her hands in his. "You look fabulous," he declared. A security guard had drifted over toward them and Jagger turned to the guy. "Have you ever seen Emily look so fantastic?"

The guard, Horace Lighterman, grinned and nodded at her. "You do look great tonight, Miss Grainger."

Okay, so the male half of the human race had all gone mad. But she was willing to roll with that. Especially if by some strange miracle the madness included her suddenly being perceived as cute. Or even hot.

In keeping with the party spirit of the evening, she replied playfully, "Thanks, Horace. You're looking pretty spiffy yourself. I love the hat." The guy had on a pointed cardboard affair that looked utterly ridiculous with his police-style uniform. The silliness of the combination somehow poked fun at AbaCo, and she found that immensely appealing. Her employer could stand to be ridiculed now and then. Any other day of the year, Horace wouldn't have dared to wear that hat, and she wouldn't have dared to find it funny. But New Year's Eve was about letting loose. About taking chances. About new starts.

Someone called for Horace from the security desk just inside the lobby and he turned away from them.

"Come on," Jagger announced. "Let's go have fun."

Let's? As in him and her? As in wow. There must be definite magic in the air tonight. Either that or a hallucinogen in the water supply.

They'd barely stepped into the atrium proper when there was a ruckus behind her. Several plainclothed AbaCo security guards clustered at the front door, looking like angry wasps. One of them was holding what looked like a black backpack.

"Dance with me," Jagger announced, more of a command than a question.

His arms went around her and he swept her into a waltz, spinning her effortlessly across the dance floor. Most of the couples dancing were older, executive types. She recognized several vice presidents and their wives, and frankly, she felt a little funny out here with them. But Jagger was such a spectacular partner that she rapidly lost all self-consciousness.

He guided her exactly where she needed to be, kept her precisely on the beat and whisked her around the room like Cinderella. Who knew waltzing could be so much fun?

She wasn't sure what made her dizzy. It could have been the swooping, turning flight he took her on around the dance floor, or maybe it was the way he smiled down at her—as if she were the only person in the entire world and the two of them were alone at their own private ball. Either way, it was pretty sensational.

The dance ended, and he walked her off the floor, steering her toward the bar and a cool drink as if he could read her mind. She sipped at the gin and tonic he brought her. She never drank under normal circumstances. But in the past ten minutes, she'd already established that tonight was anything *but* normal.

"How come I haven't seen you around here before?" she asked curiously. Which was to say, how on earth had she missed spotting or at least hearing about a hunk like him if they worked in the same building?

He laughed easily. "I was just thinking the very same thing about you."

"Ah, well. I work in my little cubicle most of the time. They hardly let me come up for air, let alone poke my nose outside of the Special Cargo Department."

His gaze flickered, but his smile never faltered. He murmured, "Let's not talk about work tonight, shall we? Tell me more about you."

She rolled her eyes. "I guarantee you, I have led the most boring life in the history of mankind."

"A woman who wears shoes like those? I find that very hard to believe."

She laughed. "Busted. I never wear shoes like this. They were an impulse buy. Pure foolishness."

"I like the impulse."

His eyes sparkled with laughter, but his voice slid across her skin like forbidden sex. It sent a shudder through her that bordered on orgasmic. This wasn't happening to her! She looked up at him, perplexed.

"What?" he asked, immediately serious.

"Are you for real?"

One eyebrow lifted and the devil-may-care grin was back. "Does it matter? Or shall we both just lose ourselves in the moment and see where it leads us?"

A very James Bond-like response. No wonder the Bond girls never held out for a long-term commitment from him. He was so attractive they were willing to settle for a night or two with him rather than never be with him at all. Of course, the possibility of something more than a one-night stand wasn't off the table between her and Jagger yet, either. Heck, she was thrilled that the prospect of a one-night stand was even on the table!

Which was to say, the world had definitely gone mad this New Year's Eve.

She sipped her drink and smiled back at him coyly. "The night *is* young, isn't it? Let's see where it goes, indeed."

Chapter 2

Jagger was staggered by Emily Grainger. Not in his wildest dreams would he have guessed that a parka could unwrap to reveal this jewel. She was perfect. And scary as hell. He didn't go for real women, the hearth-and-home kind a guy could envision having his babies and keeping a home with. Oh, no. She was not his type at all.

So why, then, was he so attracted to her he could hardly keep his hands off her?

Not good. Not good at all.

The first thing he noticed about her was her flawless, translucent skin. Contrasted against her lush brunette hair, the combination was beyond striking. Her eyes were big and dark, her lips ripe for the kissing. He preferred her rosy mouth after the first gin and tonic lifted away that pale pink lipstick. She looked eminently more kissable now.

But what absolutely blew him away was the look of delighted wonder in her eyes. Her gaze was so innocent, so guileless, so…pure, he almost felt inappropriate touching her. In his world, the people were hard. Cynical. Out to stab you in the back before you stabbed them. All the playfulness, all the innocence had been burned out of men like him—of him—long ago. But she had both. In spades. And they drew him in as effortlessly as a spider coaxing a fly into its web. The world's most innocent spider.

He'd accuse her of being childlike if it weren't for the intelligence lurking just below the surface of that warm chocolate gaze. He could all but hear the wheels turning as she processed and analyzed everything and everyone around her. It was a strange dichotomy. But no doubt about it, he sensed a first-class mind at work.

Thankfully, she seemed in total ignorance of men like him, however.

His mouth turned down cynically. He was a user. He took what he needed from the people around him and then threw them away like so much discarded trash. A girl like Emily certainly deserved better than that. But as sure as God made little green apples, he was going to use her anyway. It was who he was. He didn't know how to do anything else.

But a warning vibrated deep in his gut. This woman might leave an indelible mark on him. She was a permanent kind of woman who could shake the very foundation of his impermanent world.

He yanked his mind back to the job at hand. If and when the AbaCo security team finally relaxed a little, he'd sneak off and make his way up an elevator and into the offices above. He'd break into the company's computers and download everything he could find on the company's shipping operations. And hopefully, somewhere in there, they'd find a lead on his missing fellow agents. If he was really lucky, his colleagues would find something criminal with which to charge AbaCo and launch a wider investigation of the secretive company's practices.

But until that moment when he had to bail out on her, he could make this a night to remember for Emily Grainger. It was the least he owed her for her unwitting help. Not to mention, he seemed compelled to flirt with the danger this woman represented to him. He fed her compliments, laughed with her and did his very best Prince Charming imitation for her.

As she continued to dance and talk with him, he plied her with equal parts alcohol and enticement until her eyes blazed with utter infatuation. And somewhere along the way, his plan of attack changed. Why ditch Emily after a few hours to take a one-shot stab at breaking in tonight when he could play out this thing between them and potentially turn her into a long-term infiltrator of AbaCo from the inside?

Hypocrite. He just wanted an excuse to spend more time with the girl.

No, dammit, that wasn't all this was about. It was good business to turn the girl.

Nonetheless, his gut twinged. Did he have it in him to make a pawn out of sweet, trusting Emily? Hell, a woman like her should never look twice at a man like him. He really should warn her off. But he couldn't bring himself to do it. God, he was a jerk. He didn't deserve Emily Grainger.

"Are you okay?" A soft hand rested on his chest, jolting him back to the present. Damn, she was perceptive.

He grinned bleakly at her. "Yeah, sure. I was just pondering what New Year's resolution I should make this year."

"Hmm. That's a good question." Laughter twinkled in her warm gaze. "Mine is going to be to wear more red shoes."

"Gonna take more chances, huh? Gonna try living on the edge?" he teased. The thought of her existing in a world like his was ludicrous. But he couldn't begrudge her the dream, he supposed. The reality was so much darker than a woman like her could ever imagine.

She nodded firmly. "Yup. That's me. Danger Girl."

He laughed, genuinely amused. She had no idea just how dangerous to him she was. He commented lightly, "Well, then, my resolution is to help you make your resolution come true."

Her gaze snapped to his. Not slow on the uptake, his Emily. She hadn't for a minute missed the implications of that. He was talking about continuing to see her after tonight. He looked her in the eyes, losing himself in their sweet depths. To have a woman like this for himself, to bathe himself in all that goodness, to soak up her innocence and generosity, to be loved forever by someone like her—

He cut the fantasy off cold. Danger Girl, indeed.

"Wanna take a walk?" she murmured. "Get a little fresh air?"

He grinned. "I think that's supposed to be my line. Then comes the part where I drag you into some dark corner and try to make out with you."

She grinned back. "Who says I'm not trying to drag you into the corner to make out with you?"

He nodded his amused acquiescence. "Lead on. My body is yours to ravage."

He was shocked when she led him over to the elevators and punched the up button. She wasn't going to take him up to her office—in the Special Cargo Department, no less—was she? Surely this op wouldn't be *that* easy.

He leaned down to murmur in her ear, "Are you planning to throw me down on your desk and have your way with me?"

A fiery blush leaped to her cheeks. "Good Lord, my cubicle will never be the same now that you've planted *that* image in my mind!"

"Think how much fun work's going to be on Monday morning," he teased.

"I was thinking that we could go out to the water garden and stroll around."

Ah. The building's tenth floor was not a floor at all. Rather it was an open-air terrace sporting massive columns and housing an elaborate outdoor modern art collection interspersed with, as she'd already alluded to, a bunch of fountains. All the good stuff in the firm was above that. It was the reason he'd come in through the roof—or at least tried to until that plan went completely to hell.

The elevator opened, and she punched a security code into the number pad inside. He memorized the six-digit number as a matter of course. Emily Grainger was the brass ring and then some for getting the inside scoop on AbaCo. She so far surpassed his wildest expectations for this op that he could hardly believe his luck. And all he could do was imagine different ways to bed her. He was a cad. A sharp knife of guilt stabbed him.

While he admonished himself to get over it and concentrate on his job, she reached out shyly to loop her fingers in the crook of his elbow. He gazed down at her intently and the smile faded from her face. She stared back at him, her pupils dilating until her eyes went black as she correctly interpreted his expression.

The elevator dinged and the door slid open.

She shook herself free of their mutual reverie first and stepped toward the exit. Rocked at the effect she had on him, he followed her outside. The wind was howling tonight, but glass panels mounted at intervals all around the edge of the terrace shielded the garden from the worst of it. Nonetheless, he took off his jacket and draped it over her shoulders.

He caught the surreptitious sniff she took, inhaling his scent. And something moved deep within him. Something protective. Possessive.

They'd only walked a dozen steps forward before he spotted the first surveillance camera. This place was a freaking fortress, all right. All the more reason to give up on a simple break-in tonight. Better to cultivate Emily as a long-term asset, to spy for him from the inside.

Distracted by thoughts of all those secret meetings they'd need to have with each other, he ducked his head away from the camera out of long habit, and immediately could've kicked himself for having done it. Dammit. If the camera operator was half as good as the rest of the AbaCo team, Jagger had just sent a big red flag up the pole. No innocent civilian reacted that way to a surveillance camera. But a spy most certainly would.

He sighed. Nothing to do now but brazen it out. "Are you warm enough?" He smiled down at Emily.

"It is chilly. But I enjoy the quiet."

He wrapped an arm around her shoulder, tucking her close against his side. "Better?"

"Mmm," she murmured. She sounded like a kitten after lapping up a bowl of warm milk. "Are *you* warm enough?"

He chuckled. "I love cold weather. This is bracing."

She shook her head. "Give me a tropical beach every day of the week and twice on Sunday."

"I gathered that from the way you were bundled up when you arrived."

She laughed ruefully. "My mom always told me to dress like I expect my car to break down and be stranded for hours. I confess I have been known as a compulsive safety girl before. But no more, of course. I'm Danger Girl now."

He heard the whoosh of an elevator door behind him and held himself still, not reacting. He studied a red metal abstract sculpture in front of him. "That looks like a Calder," he commented, ignoring the guards he felt approaching in the sudden twitchiness of his shoulder blades.

"I think it is. I'm not too much into modern art, I'm afraid. I like my art old—and the subject identifiable."

He laughed quietly as two pairs of footsteps became audible.

"You there!" a male voice called out sharply.

He and Emily turned as a single unit, which had the effect of making the maneuver look nice and casual. "Can we help you?" Jagger asked smoothly.

The two men halted, eyeing him suspiciously. "How did you two get up here?"

Emily laughed. "We crawled up the side of the building using our supersuction fingers and spider silk. We took the elevator, of course."

"Who's the gentleman with you, Miss Grainger?"

Emily glanced up at him in surprise. "Why, Jagger Holtz, of course."

The men frowned. "Mind if we see a little identification, sir?"

He frowned as any innocent man would at such a request, but shrugged. "Not at all." As he dug out his wallet and passed over his driver's license, he asked, "May I ask what this is all about?"

"Routine security check, sir. Would you mind coming with us?"

His frown deepened as he swore mentally. He'd had such a good thing going with Emily, and now he was going to have to run again. And this time without a rope. He let his arm drop off Emily's shoulder and he tensed to charge the two men. He'd take the smaller one on the right first and spin him into his bigger, more dangerous-looking buddy.

Emily spoke up without warning. "Actually, we would mind. Mr. Holtz and I are trying to enjoy our New Year's Eve here. There's no law against walking around the water garden."

The bigger one replied, "We've had a security breach tonight, and we're looking for a man dressed in all black and matching the general height and build of your...friend."

"I see," she replied frostily, shrugging off Jagger's coat and handing it back to him. "Now *you* can see that my friend is not wearing all black. He was merely being a gentleman and loaning me his coat."

God bless her. He couldn't have asked for a better cover story if he'd prepped her himself.

The smaller guard opened his mouth, but Jagger interrupted him, impatiently now. The average innocent guy with a few drinks in him and a hot chick beside him would be getting all kinds of irritated, so he let a hint of testosterone-induced posturing creep into the exchange. "The lady and I arrived together. You can ask Horace down at the front desk."

The smaller guard glowered but murmured into his coat collar. The reply was swift. A finger to his ear and the guard nodded reluctantly at his partner. Both looked more than a little disgruntled. "Horace remembers the two of you arriving. Sorry to bother you.

Have a nice night." With that, the guards turned and left.

Emily complained, "I know this place can be a police state, but good grief."

Jagger steered her toward the elevator. "Let's go back inside. You're shivering."

"It's not the cold. It's those thugs. They give me the creeps."

"You're going to have to get used to facing down thugs if you want to live a life of adventure and mayhem, Danger Girl."

"I don't need mayhem. Just some naughty shoes and a little adventure with a hot guy now and then."

His lips curved upward. Hot, was he?

They rode the elevator down to the party in silence. In a single sweeping glance of the room, he spotted no less than twelve men with earpieces carrying themselves like more of Emily's thugs. The back of his neck started to tingle. He didn't like how they were arrayed around the room. It looked for all the world like an ambush about to be sprung. With him as the main course. Time to blow this popsicle stand.

Smiling casually for the thugs' benefit, he murmured, "Speaking of adventure, what say we relocate this party to someplace less thug-infested?"

She looked up at him in surprise. "What did you have in mind?"

"How about my place? We can take your car and that way you can leave whenever you want." In his experience, the safer a woman felt about her ability to leave a place, the more she was inclined to stay. He added, "I don't need all these security guys eyeing me like I'm some criminal for the next two hours."

She glanced around. "Good point."

"No pressure, Em. Just a bottle of champagne and a bite to eat. I don't expect any more than that."

She blinked up at him, her mouth and eyes round. Was she so innocent that it actually hadn't occurred to her that he might be propositioning her for sex when he invited her to his place?

She nodded in sudden decision. "As my first act of daring in the almost new year, I, Danger Girl, accept your invitation. Let's go."

He grinned, enormously relieved. He dared not let her leave his side until he was well clear of this place, lest the security team swoop in and grab him. He picked up both of their coats, and he made a humorous production of mummifying her in her scarf, hat, parka and mittens. It culminated with her sticking her tongue out at him and yanking her scarf up over her face. Ah, sweet Emily. She had no idea what a good act she was putting on for the cameras. He could kiss her.

Hell, he could kiss her and it wouldn't have a damned thing to do with AbaCo's uptight security team.

The two of them took the elevator down to the parking garage and walked quickly to her car. He never once glanced in the direction of the pillar where he'd stashed his gear earlier. He hadn't spotted a camera, but there undoubtedly was one down here. And just as undoubtedly, someone was watching for his reaction to the hiding place of the suspicious backpack the security team had found earlier.

"The roads aren't in great shape. Would you like me to drive?" he offered. "I have a lot of experience on ice."

"Uh, okay," she replied. He opened her door for her and then went around to the driver's side of her car. He eased the vehicle out of the parking space and started up the ramp.

"Where'd you learn to drive on ice?" she asked.

He couldn't very well tell her about his numerous illegal forays into Russia. "Alaska," he replied blandly. In point of fact, he'd done some Arctic training up there that had happened to include some offensive driving classes. Doing donuts on sheet ice was a kick for the first dozen revolutions or so. Then it just made a guy sick to his stomach.

"Cool. I've always wanted to go there," she said brightly.

"So take a vacation there this year, Danger Girl."

She looked over at him, her eyes sparkling like diamonds. "Maybe I will."

He maneuvered confidently through the traffic, wary of drunks. But it wasn't midnight yet, and the majority of partygoers wouldn't hit the highways for another couple of hours. He turned the heat up full blast, and it had the desired effect. Before long, Emily had shed most of her outer layers. The view was much better now. Despite how slender she was, she had a nicely proportioned cleavage, not huge, but full and round and tempting.

"Wow. You *are* a good driver," she commented.

"It's all about being decisive and knowing what your tires can do."

Silence fell between them and he pulled out his cell phone, dialed his hotel one-handed and asked for room service. When a female voice came on the line, he responded, "This is Mr. Holtz from room 2467. I'd like surf and turf for two in my room with all the trimmings, plus the Dom Perignon 1983. And a dark chocolate fondue for dessert. Extra strawberries, please.

I'll be arriving at the hotel in a half hour. Anytime after that will be fine."

He disconnected the call. Emily was staring at him as if he'd grown a third eye in the middle of his forehead. "What?" he asked.

"Are you sure you're not James Bond?"

Okay, then. That cut a little too close for comfort. He kept forgetting that beneath her playful innocence lay an intelligent and observant woman. He laughed lightly. "Thanks for the comparison. I'm afraid I'm just a regular guy."

Emily wondered about that, though. Jagger danced like a god, handled a car like a Formula One driver and ordered fancy midnight dinners as if they were an everyday occurrence in his world. Why wasn't she surprised when he pulled up in front of one of the ritziest hotels in Denver, flipped the car keys to a valet and casually passed her the ticket for her car?

As he escorted her through the lobby his hand came to rest in the small of her back, and he leaned in close as though he was claiming possession of her to any and all who looked. That crazy electricity thing happened again, and it was all she could do to walk across the lobby without falling on her face. Honestly. It was enough to turn a girl's head.

Enough to make her willing to bust out of her shell and try to become the kind of woman this man might want for longer than one night.

Of course, his room turned out to be a suite with a magnificent view of Denver and the black void of the mountains looming in the distance. Nothing but the best for Jagger Holtz, no, sir. So where did that leave her? Tonight's consolation prize? Except he hadn't even looked at another woman at the party. She'd barely taken her eyes off him all evening. She'd have noticed if he was checking the room for other fish.

She was Danger Girl, dammit. She was not about to let her complete lack of self-confidence overtake her now. She'd come this far… she could go the rest of the way toward making years' worth of fantasies come true.

Jagger took her ridiculous coat from her and

hung it up in the front closet while she wandered over to the window to admire the view. She flung the question over her shoulder, "Why me? You could've had any woman in the place tonight."

He strolled up behind her, hands fisted in his pockets. He stopped just behind her shoulder, gazing at her reflection in the black window. "Why not you?" he countered. "You're beautiful, charming, intelligent, fun, an interesting conversationalist."

She got hung up on the very first adjective. "Beautiful? Me? I don't think so."

"Beauty's in the eye of the beholder," he murmured. "I find you positively magnificent." Tension suddenly poured from him. "Emily," he half whispered, "I can't take my eyes off you." The words sounded torn unwillingly from his gut.

"But *why?*"

It was as if she'd dug one layer too deep and hit a nerve. The deep restlessness that she sensed ingrained in him went still. His body froze for a moment. His face went blank. It was as if his entire being just…shut down.

It took him several seconds to look up at her reflection and smile crookedly at it. "Can't you just accept my…compulsion to be with you…at face value?"

He had a compulsion? To be with her? Cool. As long as it didn't turn out to be some sick obsession. Although he hadn't given her the slightest hint of any aberrant impulses.

Their dinner arrived, and he lit the tall white candles between their silver-covered plates. The candlelight twinkled off the shiny sterling flatware, lending an unbearably romantic air to the table and to the entire room. He extinguished the other lights until only the twin candles lit the room, leaving the space mysterious and sexy around them.

Jagger murmured, "Like most women, you look ravishing by candlelight."

She smiled widely. "Like most women, I know it's all about the lighting and not me."

"Untrue. Even the most perfect of lighting

can only improve mediocrity so much. You're beautiful, candles or no candles."

She sighed. "You're so good for a girl's ego."

"I try," he murmured as he reached for her plate with a pair of lobster pliers.

He served her himself, pulling her lobster from the shell and even ladling dressing onto her salad for her. How was a girl supposed to resist all this pampering? By the bottom of her second glass of champagne, she was beginning to wonder why she should try. And then the fondue arrived. He fed her chocolate-dipped ladyfingers, red raspberries the size of her thumb and strawberries. Mmm, the strawberries. They were decadent.

By the bottom of the third glass of champagne, all thoughts of resisting his charms had flown right out of her head. And yet all he did after the meal was put on a smooth jazz CD and commence dancing with her. Not the big, flashy waltz of before but rather a slow and subtle swaying, just the two of them, body to body. It was…nice. Okay, maybe not nice. More like naughty. Luscious. Sexy. Fabulous.

His restraint made her feel safe. In control. And yet a little voice in the back of her head told her she was already wildly out of control. But hey. Tonight was all about taking chances.

"What kind of accounting work do you do?" he murmured as they continued to talk about anything and everything.

"I track special shipments and document the money trail from pickup to delivery."

"What kind of stuff constitutes a special shipment?"

She smiled up at him. "I don't ask, and the clients don't tell. Stuff in boxes, mostly. Commercial containers. Usually heavy and sealed airtight." She shrugged. "I figure it's illegal arms shipments."

"Seriously?" he blurted.

She laughed. "No, I'm joking of course. I have no idea what it is. I just make sure it's paid for and gets there on time."

"Do you do anything else?"

"Well, sure. Sometimes they need me to do other stuff."

"What kind of stuff?"

"You know. Exciting stuff. Like order food and toilet paper for ship crews. Or relay the fuel load a ship plans to take on when it comes into port." Her tongue wasn't cooperating quite as well as she'd like, and rather than sound tipsy, she threw the conversation back in his lap. "What do you do?"

"Stuff." He laughed down at her.

"I don't suppose I have to ask anyway. Everybody knows what James Bond does."

He laughed under his breath. "Are we talking about in the bedroom or out of it?"

She giggled up at him. The bubbles from the champagne had definitely gone to her head. "Personally, I think ol' James was a little deficient in that department."

Jagger's eyes popped wide open. "How so?"

"Well, think about it. All those women, and not a one of them ever got pregnant. And you have to admit, he isn't the kind of man who'd have a vasectomy. He's too macho to be that responsible. Which means—" she sighed for dramatic effect "—that the legendary Double-O-Seven shoots blanks. If you catch my meaning." She waggled her eyebrows exaggeratedly just to make sure.

Jagger all but doubled over in laughter, and she puffed up at the notion that he was laughing at her. "What's so funny?" she demanded.

"That an innocent kitten like you actually thinks about such things."

"I'm not innocent," she asserted indignantly. "Far from it."

He drew her closer, murmuring, "Hmm. That remains to be seen."

Not to be distracted from the subject at hand, she mused, "I suppose if a girl was looking for a sperm donor to give her a baby, James Bond wouldn't be a bad candidate—if all the equipment worked, of course. He's smart, handsome, charming, accomplished…" She batted her eyelashes up at him.

Jagger rolled his eyes. "I highly doubt James thought that far ahead. Guys like him live in the moment. They don't even think about surviving beyond the current mission."

"You say that like you know something about it."

"Not me," he replied blandly.

They danced in silence for several more minutes, and then he abruptly strode over to the television and turned it on. A timer was counting down the final seconds to the new year. She'd completely lost track of time in his arms.

Three. Two. One.

"Happy New Year," he murmured…

…and then he kissed her.

Chapter 3

Emily gasped. From the first moment their lips touched, it was *magic*. It was as if she'd been waiting for him all her life and, having now found him, had known him deep in her bones forever. He lifted his mouth away from hers and her eyes fluttered open.

He was staring down at her. In open shock, if she wasn't mistaken.

"Wow." Her heart was having no part of beating normally.

He cleared his throat. "Yeah. What you said."

She laughed in wonder. Happy New Year, indeed.

And then he all but inhaled her. Of course, she all but inhaled him back. The explosion of lust between them was instant and hotter than the sun. It sizzled across her skin, searing away everything in its path, every consideration of why not to jump into bed with him, every ounce of common sense, everything but him. Just him.

She needed him just as she needed to breathe. More.

"What have you done to me?" he muttered against her neck as he bent down to reach for the hem of her dress.

The slinky fabric slid off her body with a sexy glide of fabric on flesh. "I don't know, but you did it to me, too." She fumbled at the hem of his turtleneck, tugging it over his head to reveal a chest fully as gorgeous as hinted at under his clothing. "Do it some more," she urged.

His laugh was low and charged.

Score one for Danger Girl. Heck, score a million. Game over, Danger Girl won this round, hands down. Why, oh, why hadn't she discovered this side of herself years ago? How could she have hidden in the pink cocoon of her safe little world for so long? She'd never dreamed *this* was out there waiting for her. A man like Jagger. This wild pleasure that was a fire in her blood.

The rest of their clothes came off quickly, and the lights went off, leaving only the twin candles still guttering over the remains of their supper. An alto saxophone wailed a smoky blues tune from the stereo, and the air was redolent of chocolate, deep and dark and rich.

He carried her to the bed, laying her upon it and then standing back to look at her. Normally, she'd be absolutely mortified to be examined naked by a man she barely knew. Except this was Jagger. And Danger Girl thought it was glorious to have him look at her like this, as if she was his and he was never letting go of her. Maybe it was just the champagne. Or maybe he brought out the brazen hussy in her. But either way, she wasn't about to cower in front of this man. She wanted him. All of him. She planned to act out every naughty fantasy she'd ever had, tonight.

She held out her arms to him. "Come here, you."

He didn't wait for her to ask twice. He placed

a knee on the bed beside her. Then he did a slow-motion press down to her, stopping when their mouths were a hairsbreadth apart.

"Are you sure about this?" he murmured. "No pressure. If you want to stop, just tell me."

She laughed and scowled up at him. "Don't you dare stop."

"As the lady commands." He sank the rest of the way down to her, gathering her close and rolling onto his side. They snuggled for a moment while he seemed to simply savor the feel of her against him. She appreciated the fact that he wasn't in any rush. That he could take his time and savor every bit of this experience. No green boy was Jagger Holtz, no, sir. He made her feel as though she was in good hands. Confident hands. Hands that were starting to roam up and down her spine and do the most delicious things to her entire body. Who'd have guessed so many nerves in so many places were hot-wired directly to her backbone?

She couldn't help it. She wriggled impatiently against him.

His chuckle tickled her ear, and he seemed to know the time for teasing her was over. "Show me what you want, Emily."

And then all that heat and urgency and muscle were hers. She wrapped herself around him like a freezing person embracing a roaring furnace. She kissed his chest, his neck, his jaw. And all the while, his hands roamed over her body, skimming across her skin and leaving a trail of utter destruction in their wake.

He shoved her hands up against the headboard and slid down her body as her urgency increased, driving her crazy with his mouth. He muttered, "What am I going to do with you? This is madness, but damned if I can stop it."

"More," she managed to gasp. "I want more."

She arched up into him, shuddering uncontrollably as his blazing mouth closed on her. He worked his way back up her body, incinerating everything that was left of her. Only then did he plunge into the very core of her, groaning his pleasure.

Their twin suns went supernova then, combusting so bright and hot that the explosion defied comprehension. They rode the incendiary wave, blasting outward from their cores on a solar storm that reached far out into the cosmos, finally flinging them into a void so silent and peaceful, Emily wasn't sure she was still alive.

"You've killed me," Jagger breathed.

She managed to gather enough breath to laugh. "I was thinking the very same thing."

"Well, then, I think we've established that you are no innocent, Ms. Grainger."

"Just call me Danger Girl."

"Right. And a more apt name there never was. You are more than dangerous, my dear. You're lethal."

"I hope you mean that in a good way," she chuckled.

"Indubitably."

"Thanks, Double-O-Seven."

His answering smile was serene. Contented. "You're welcome. And thank you."

He pulled her across his chest, draping her over his body until they were joined practically as one. His heart still pounded like a jackhammer beneath her ear, belying his outward calm. Had she done that to him? Cool.

She smiled in utter contentment of her own. How had she ever lived without him in her life? This was more than love at first sight. Was there such a thing as soul mates at first sight?

No doubt about it. She'd break out of whatever shell she must to keep this man. She'd move heaven and earth to be with him.

His lips moved in her hair. "You probably won't believe me, but this sort of thing doesn't happen to me often."

Her answer was prompt. "You're right. I don't believe you."

He laughed. "I'm serious."

She made a colossal effort and lifted her head enough to gaze at him. "You're telling me a man like you can't have any woman he wants anytime?"

He laughed. "I don't *want* any woman anytime. I have my standards, you know." He pressed a finger against her mouth as if he knew she'd ask how in the world she possibly met his standards. "But you…you're incredible, Emily. I think you've ruined me for any other woman."

She laughed. "Now I know you're lying. But thanks. That's sweet of—"

His mouth swooped down on hers, and he kissed her with such passion she completely lost the rest of the thought. When she was breathless and clinging to him in panting need, he whispered, "I mean it. You…you're… magic."

She knew the feeling exactly.

He continued, murmuring contemplatively, "Would you think I was weird if I said I feel like I've been looking for you for a very long time?"

"Not if you promise not to think I'm weird for thinking the very same thing."

Their laughter mingled as they stared out into the cold night outside the windows. She couldn't imagine anything more perfect than being here with him, right now, in the relaxed afterglow of their lovemaking. She couldn't ever recall being more warm and content than she was in this exact second. The peace of it reached deep into her soul. She would never forget this moment as long as she lived. It was perfect. Exactly, totally perfect.

Would he disappear come tomorrow, like James Bond? Would he give her time to become Danger Girl in truth? She doubted most people got even one moment of happiness this pure in their lives, let alone a lifetime of it. Was she greedy to want more? Not that it mattered. She already knew she wouldn't be able stop herself from trying to hold on to him for as long as she could.

The next time they made love it was slow and lazy, filled with long kisses and intimate whispers. She savored every second of it, doing her darnedest to make a lasting memory of every millisecond. To wrap each piece of it carefully in her mind and pack it away in her heart's treasure chest. It reminded her of what a honeymoon must feel like. Or a wedding night.

The thought gave her a jolt, and Jagger whispered against her collarbone, "What?"

"Mmm, nothing. Just random delicious thoughts."

She felt his lips curve into a smile on her skin. He murmured, "You're delicious. Entirely edible."

She chuckled. "I thought we'd already established that."

"Yes, but," he disagreed, "we haven't yet established how you taste with chocolate fondue."

Her gaze snapped over to the fondue pot still warming on the table. "Oh, my."

In the wee hours of the morning, as she lay limp and utterly sated, she curled into the circle of his arms and knew, without a shadow of a doubt, this was the one place in the entire world she'd most like to be. Forever.

She was home. Danger Girl had found The One.

And with that thought in mind, she finally drifted off to sleep, dreaming of naughty red shoes and chocolate.

Jagger woke up feeling more refreshed in body, mind and soul than he had in years.

And the cause of it was buried beneath a pile of blankets with little but her nose sticking out from under the covers. And what a lovely nose it was. He smiled indulgently. Emily might run cold when she was asleep, but she'd been plenty hot enough last night to burn him alive.

To hell with caution. So what if she was a forever girl and he was a one-night guy? She'd become his AbaCo informant and they'd work together for a good long time. Long enough to work this fever for her out of his blood and get back to being the one-night guy his work—his life—demanded of him.

He spied an empty champagne bottle on the coffee table. He hoped she didn't feel the aftereffects of the bubbly too bad this morning. But just in case, he ought to order up a pot of coffee. Except he didn't have the heart to wake her just yet. It had been a very long night, and she deserved to sleep in nice and late.

Still, he could use some caffeine. He slipped out of bed quietly, pulled on jeans and a sweatshirt and grabbed his ski jacket. He'd just run down to the corner and get them some fresh lattes and muffins. He'd be back long before she stirred, let alone woke up.

The temperature had dropped below zero overnight, and this first day of the new year nipped at his cheeks and forehead with sharp teeth. The streets weren't exactly deserted this Sunday morning, but they weren't far from it. He jammed his hands in his pockets, hunched his collar up around his ears and set out for the coffee shop a block from the hotel.

He'd bet she liked her coffee turned into virtual ice cream with cream and sugar. He'd buy her one of every flavor of muffin, too—

Something stung him sharply in the neck, as painfully as a wasp. Oww!

He reached up reflexively to slap at the spot, and he lurched as someone grabbed him from behind. He reacted fast and hard, slamming his elbow into his assailant and whipping around to bring his feet to bear in the fight as his years of martial arts training kicked in. But his elbow blow was blunted by his attacker's thickly padded jacket, and whatever had been in the needle in his neck was damned fast acting. The street blurred and swam woozily before his eyes. *Crap. I'm in deep trouble here.*

Something huge and dark screeched to a halt at his side and three more men leaped out of the van to surround him. It was no contest. His legs were already collapsing out from underneath him. Frantically, he looked around for help. Even a simple witness to report his capture to the police. But the attack had been perfectly timed. Not a soul was in sight, let alone within shouting range.

His vision narrowed down to a gray tunnel and then to a single pinprick of light.

"Emily…" he gasped.

And then everything went black.

Chapter 4

Two years later

Jagger huddled in the tiny room, hugging his knees, drawing the darkness close around him like a security blanket. At least they were leaving him alone more these days. That was better than the constant interrogations and beatings of his first few months of captivity. But sometimes, in the dark of this endless night, he got so damned lonely he almost wished for the thugs to come back. Worse than decent food, worse than a real shower, worse almost than freedom, he craved human company. Someone to talk to him. Just normal, meaningless conversations about normal, meaningless things.

But he doubted his life would ever be normal again. Eventually, he'd catch some disease, or he'd become malnourished, or maybe he'd just give up on living. Then he was a goner. And not a damned soul would know or care. He figured his captors would push his entire crate overboard into the middle of the ocean and call it good. No more Jagger Holtz.

What kind of life was it to have lived where no one would give a crap if he died? There ought to be someone to care. But that would've meant having someone permanent in his life. Like Emily Grainger. A forever woman. But people in his line of work didn't do long-term relationships. At least not often, and generally not well.

If only he had someone to look forward to going home to. Maybe that would help him endure this unending nightmare.

He glanced at the hole he'd punctured in the corner of his crate when he was first thrown into this shipping container to rot. It served as his only marker of the passage of time. Darkness had fallen outside. Another day gone, which made this the seven hundred twenty-eighth day of his captivity. And that would make tomorrow…he checked the math and a bitter laugh rose up in his chest…New Year's Eve. Again.

For the thousandth time, he relived that fateful New Year's Eve two years ago. He should've seen the signs. His instincts should've warned him. But he'd been so besotted with Emily Grainger he'd never seen the trap coming. He'd let his guard down. Gotten distracted by a woman. No wonder James Bond never let himself fall for any of his many conquests. Ol' James understood the dangers of losing focus, apparently. Lucky bastard.

One thing he knew for sure. If he ever got out of here, if he ever found the people who'd put him into this hellhole, he was going to kill them all. Slowly and painfully.

Emily winced and looked back over her shoulder at yet another AbaCo facility festooned with those awful metallic Christmas decorations. They must be regulation company issue. At least this office had the advantage of being in paradise. She'd leaped at the opportunity to take this exotic position when it had come along. All part and parcel of her campaign to become Danger Girl for real. Jagger Holtz might have run out on her, but she would never forget how he'd made her feel. She'd been fully alive for the first time. She couldn't ever go back to the way she'd been before, Jagger or no Jagger.

The Hawaii AbaCo office occupied its own private island at the far western end of the chain of one hundred thirty-seven atolls, islets and islands that made up the Hawaiian archipelago. Although it was more of a refueling depot than an actual office. The Rock, as most of the employees called it, boasted a deepwater dock and underground fuel-storage and pumping facilities, plus a small collection of buildings.

Oddly, the staff numbered close to sixty, even though the lone office building here could probably only hold half that number—standing up and tightly packed. Two dozen longshoremen refueled and resupplied the ships, and the security team accounted for another dozen of the tall, silent men on the payroll. She was told that AbaCo put divers in the water for security purposes whenever one of its container ships came into port, which supposedly accounted for most of the rest of the powerful-looking men that made up the staff.

But in the time she'd been here, the actual work getting done and the number of able-bodied men stationed here to do it didn't add up. There always seemed to be spare guys hanging around the small AbaCo building, going in and out of Kurt Schroder's office for hush-hush meetings. He was the site manager.

He'd seemed surprised when she'd shown up, letters of introduction in hand from the North American chief of security for AbaCo. But after Schroder read the letter, he merely shrugged and showed her to a desk. Her job here wasn't so different from what she'd done in Denver. It mostly entailed tracking shipments, making sure they got to where they were supposed to go on time, that the money got into the right accounts and answering a few phones.

The staff rotated in and out of this remote location. Two weeks on the Rock, two weeks off-duty on a Hawaiian island of personal choice. She'd chosen Kauai. It was everything she'd imagined Hawaii to be and more—tropical, lush and laid-back. She'd fallen in love with it from the first moment she'd set foot on it.

She'd even talked her mother into moving out here with her on this once-in-a-lifetime assignment to hold down the fort at the Kauai condo during the times Emily was posted on the Rock.

"There you are," a deep male voice grumbled from behind her.

Schroder. Dang. That guy could track her down anywhere. Here she was, parked on the far side of the island from the offices, and he still showed up unannounced to check on her. It bordered on creepy. It wasn't that he had any kind of a romantic interest in her. Two years ago she might have suspected that. But now she knew better. She'd experienced true chemistry once—and she and Kurt Schroder did not have *it.*

Of course, look where having *it* with a guy had gotten her. Maybe chemistry-challenged guys were a better bet if a girl wanted some sort of sane, stable life. Still, she didn't like how Kurt was constantly popping up unannounced when she least expected him.

"There you are, Emily. Strange place to take your lunch break."

She shrugged. "I was tired. I thought a hike might wake me up. I still have a little work to do this afternoon to wind things up before the New Year's Eve party."

She winced as she said the words. Would she never get past her memories of the fateful New Year's Eve party two years ago that had so completely changed her life—changed *her?*

Schroder seemed to accept her explanation. "Be careful out here. The rocks can be treacherous, and they get slippery when it rains." He cast a grim gaze up at a low cloud bank, which was indeed threatening to wet down the tiny island. The Kona Winds were blowing today, bringing in a heavy, muggy air mass and terminally bad hair to this corner of the world.

She sighed, pushed the frizzies out of her face and followed her boss back to the shipping office. So much for a moment of privacy. A person would think that there'd be plenty of alone time to be had on an isolated rock in the middle of the Pacific Ocean, but that person would obviously have failed to figure in the pervasive eye of AbaCo always watching over its employees.

She was due to rotate off the island the day after tomorrow, and she dared not leave much by way of unfinished work for her replacement, a taciturn ex-German Army man who was about as capable with paperwork as she was with a submachine gun. Which was to say, she couldn't tell the business end of a gun from the….whatever the nonbusiness end was called.

She filed the last stack of bills of lading and had all but finished matching the latest round of payments received with their various shipments when the bell on her computer dinged to indicate an incoming e-mail. She swung her chair around to face her screen and pulled up the message.

Zhow Min. 3-6-D-15472.

What on earth? She stared at the message for several seconds trying to make sense of it. There was no greeting, no signature block. The e-mail address from which the message originated was MysteryMom. Not exactly the sort of address one of AbaCo's shipping clients was likely to use. Was this message even meant for her? Emily glanced at her screen again and saw the message was addressed to her personally and not to the AbaCo office here on the Rock.

What did it mean?

The *Zhow Min* part was obvious. A supercontainer ship by that name was due in from China sometime after midnight tonight. It was scheduled to be in port for twenty-four hours to refuel and take on supplies. The crew would lay over in the dormitory provided for that purpose until tomorrow evening.

But what were those numbers all about? She

pulled up the ship's cargo manifest on her computer and compared the numbers to the various cargo shipments on the *Zhow Min*. Nothing even remotely resembled the number sequence. Was 3-6 a date? She couldn't think of anything special about March 6, and a quick search of the Internet revealed only that it was Michaelangelo's birthday, the siege of the Alamo ended that day and aspirin was patented on that date in history.

She frowned. Who was MysteryMom, anyway? She'd never heard of the woman.

Bizarre.

She deleted the message, shut down her computer and walked slowly across the island to her room in the employees' dorm to take a nap before tonight's festivities. But the numbers continued to dance across her mind's eye, teasing her—3-6-D-15472.

The cryptic message was still tantalizing her when she finally escaped from the New Year's Eve party later that night, unable to withstand the memories it evoked any longer. Maybe a walk would help clear her mind.

Frankly, she wasn't a big puzzle kind of girl. And whoever'd sent her that message had been a tad too cryptic for her. If it was important, MysteryMom would just have to suck it up and send her something that a normal human being could comprehend. She wandered down to the island's tiny, pristine beach, letting the quiet lapping of waves soothe her troubled thoughts. It was hard to stay worked up for very long in this balmy tropical clime.

"There you are."

Jeez. Did Schroder have a tracking radio glued to her back that she didn't know about?

"Why did you leave the party?" he demanded.

As if he really cared about that. She knew darn good and well he wasn't asking because he took any kind of personal interest in her fun. He just got a kick out of controlling everyone's life around here.

She considered how to answer him. She couldn't very well complain about not being with her family when, a, everyone else out here was away from their families tonight and no one else was complaining about it, and, b, she'd volunteered for the holiday work cycle and the double overtime pay that came with it.

Reluctantly, she confessed a piece of the truth. "I'm not a big fan of tight places. And all those people crammed in that one room were a little much for me."

Schroder's gaze flickered as if he was cataloging that tidbit for future reference. Not that she could imagine where it would ever come in useful to him. He was always compiling lists of facts, neatly organized, about everything and everyone.

Schroder spoke in tones just shy of an outright order. "Come inside. The food just arrived. Bratwurst, sauerkraut, Wiener schnitzel and good German beer."

Ah. That must have been the speedboat she'd heard roar up to the pier a few minutes ago. Supplies were often brought over by boat from Lokaina, the nearest inhabited island. It lay about twenty miles away to the east and boasted not only a small permanent settlement, but even a tiny airport. It was from Lokaina Municipal Airport that workers on the Rock

shuttled to and from their homes on the big islands of Hawaii, nearly a thousand miles to the
east. Tonight's German feast had been flown in
all the way from Honolulu.

Schroder commented as she hesitated to go
back with him, "We've only got a few hours
until the *Zhow Min* arrives. Not much time to
celebrate."

Current estimated time of arrival on the ship
was sometime between 2:00 and 3:00 a.m.
Reminded of that strange e-mail message yet
again, she frowned. Schroder's brow lowered
in determination as well. He must have mis-
read her expression to mean she was planning to refuse his semiorder to go back inside.
Although she'd much rather skip the heavy
German food and stay out here to enjoy the
waves and the isolation, Schroder wasn't the
kind of man to take no for an answer. She
sighed and turned to follow him back to the
party.

The midnight meal, although tasty, was as
heavy as she'd anticipated. She was glad to
retire to the big dormitory and tumble into her

bed as soon as Schroder seemed to think it was acceptable for her to go. Except sleep wouldn't come tonight. She lay there for over an hour and finally gave up on it. Those damned numbers kept floating around in her head, taunting her with some meaning hanging just beyond her grasp.

It was probably inevitable that as 2:00 a.m. approached she felt a compulsion to get up and go for a hike around the island. And, oh, maybe she'd stroll over and have a look at the *Zhow Min* when it came in and see if those damned numbers revealed their hidden meaning to her then.

She stepped out into the humid night. She topped the spine of rock marking the center of the island and was immediately assailed by bright lights coming from the massive pier below. The *Zhow Min* was gliding the last hundred yards or so to the dock. The top-heavy ship, loaded down with rectangular steel containers in huge stacks from stem to stern, was huge and ungainly and reminded Emily of a pregnant whale. The checkerboard of colored containers—each the size of a semitruck trailer—was brightly lit under giant banks of halogen lights that turned night into day all along the pier.

Emily moved off to her right, away from glare of the lights and toward the promontory that overlooked the pier from one side. The behemoth eased the final few feet into its slip in majestic slow motion and shuddered to a halt. Lines the thickness of Emily's waist thudded ashore to moor the *Zhow Min* to pilings the size of small cars.

The same layer of clouds that had provided soft gray cover all day obscured the moon now, and the sea was black beneath the featureless sky. From this angle, the *Zhow Min* was a building-sized silhouette. One moment Emily saw nothing, and the next, she was aware of several black forms—humans—looking like tiny ants next to the gigantic ship, scaling its hull on invisible lines.

Squinting, she counted three black-garbed figures. Were they doing some sort of maintenance? She didn't remember any being scheduled, and her master database tracked such things. The men didn't seem to be pausing anywhere on the hull as if to inspect or repair it. They reached the deck and huddled, then moved off in what could be described only as stealth toward the stern of the ship. She noticed that all of them wore backpacks of some kind. The humps on their backs made the men look vaguely tortoiselike as they crept off into the shadows.

What in the world were they up to?

Then the trio did something even more strange. They commenced climbing one of the mountains of containers. The third clump back from the prow of the ship. They climbed to the fourth layer of containers, and then made their way inward six boxes, to stop at a faded green container. Bemused, she moved farther out the cliff to get a better view. The men were hard to see as they clung to the container in the deep shadows. They were definitely acting as though they didn't want to be seen.

As she looked on, the container's door slid open. Her jaw dropped as the men disappeared inside, pulling the door shut behind them. This was not a port of entry! Without Customs present, no container was allowed to be unsealed like that! What could they possibly be doing?

She stepped farther forward, craning to see what the men would do next.

A big, blond man standing on the pier beneath a bank of lights pivoted suddenly, peering in all directions. *Schroder.*

It dawned on her that she was completely exposed up here on the cliffs like this. Emily dropped to the ground, flattening herself in the shadows behind an outcropping of low stones and praying he hadn't spotted her.

As she peered out from behind the scant cover of the rocks, Schroder held his position on the pier. Surely he'd have barged up here to check out the unauthorized observer if he'd spotted her. She exhaled in relief. Nonetheless, she stayed right where she was, hidden behind her shield of black volcanic pumice.

Within a minute or two, the container door opened again. The men emerged. They retraced their steps in as much stealth as before, rappelling down the stack of containers and sprinting along the rail to where they'd left their ropes hanging overboard. Something was different about them…then it hit her. All three men had lost their backpacks. They must have left them in that container.

What could those men possibly be smuggling in AbaCo containers? A drug shipment would be more bulky than that, wouldn't it? Illegal weapons would also be bulky and heavy. Jewels would be smaller than the three backpacks. Money, maybe? That might explain it. As she pondered the possibilities, the men shimmied down the hull almost too fast for her to keep sight of, slipped below the edge of the pier and disappeared from sight.

Interestingly enough, Schroder strode off the pier then and headed back toward the office. It was almost as if he'd been acting as a lookout for the men who'd broken into that container. What was up with that? It didn't take a rocket scientist to figure out that something fishy was going on around here. The question was, could she contain her natural curiosity and steer clear of trouble as any sensible person would?

She watched the *Zhow Min* for a few more minutes, hoping to catch sight of the men once more. But they were gone. Schroder didn't return, either.

Frowning, she made a mental note of exactly where on the ship the container she'd seen them enter was located. She ought to be able to find it in the ship's load plan the next morning. She could cross-reference that with the ship's manifest and see what was in that box they'd tampered with. It was the sort of thing she might do in the course of her regular job duties. If somebody noticed her poking around, they wouldn't think anything of it.

It wasn't as though she could report what she'd seen. Schroder was clearly in on whatever was going on around here, and he was the guy she'd have to report the incident to. If and when she found evidence of anything suspicious, then she'd have to figure out if Schroder's superiors were in on the racket out here. She could always call Customs—but they'd want hard evidence, too. Better to look into the matter quietly on her own and not make any waves for now.

She turned around to head back to her bed. She'd taken maybe a dozen steps when a dark shape emerged out of the rocks ahead to loom in front of her. She lurched, violently startled. "Kurt! I didn't hear you coming!"

Schroder was maybe a dozen yards away from her, striding toward her angrily, his eyebrows slammed together furiously. "What are you doing out here?" he demanded.

She blinked, alarmed. "I couldn't sleep after all that heavy food. I came out for a bit of fresh air."

He looked over toward the *Zhow Min* and back at her suspiciously. "What are you doing up on this cliff?"

She was a lousy liar, so she stuck to the truth as much as possible. Meanwhile, alarm bells clanged wildly in her head. "I stopped for a moment to enjoy the view. She sure is a big ship, isn't she?"

"How long have you been here?"

He asked that as if there was a definite right answer and a definite wrong one. More internal alarms and sirens warned her to answer evasively, "I just got here." As he continued to eye her angrily, she added, "Too bad it's not daytime. I can't see much in the dark. I'd love to watch one of the big container ships dock."

The stiff set of his shoulders eased fractionally. "A couple more are due in next week. Take a few minutes away from your desk and watch one. It's a surprisingly delicate maneuver considering how big and clumsy those ships are."

She nodded and then said lightly, "Well, I'm off to finish my hike around the island before I turn in. Wanna come along? I'll race you back to the dorm."

"Since when are you a runner?"

"New Year's resolution to get into better shape," she replied cheerfully.

He made no comment, nor did he make any move to join her as she turned to trot back toward her room and some privacy to think about what she'd witnessed and figure out what to do about it.

* * *

The next morning, she was no closer to an answer. She opened her cargo tracking database as usual and casually typed up the manifest for the *Zhow Min.* Third stack back. Sixth column in. Fourth layer high…and then it hit her, 3-6-D. If letters were used to designate the layers of containers, that was the exact location of the container she'd seen those men climb into. The cargo manifest said the container was a climate-controlled box—commonly called a reefer in the shipping business—with a self-contained ventilation and cooling system. This particular reefer was listed as carrying salmon, caviar and live lobsters to San Francisco. Nothing to inspire a middle-of-the-night break-in there.

She frowned at her screen.

"Something wrong?" Kurt asked from the doorway as he entered the building.

Man, that guy was irritating! And his timing was freakishly good—or bad, as the case might be. She reached up to hit the clear button as she answered, "Nope. Just checking on some cargo."

He wandered into his office along with a half dozen of those oddly unemployed men who were always hanging out on the Rock and closed his door. She glared at the panel. Schroder had blocked out an hour on his daily schedule for this meeting. Plenty of time for her to stroll down to the dock and have a look at that box.

She could get in trouble…but she could always say that she was checking to make sure the refrigeration was still working and that the seafood wasn't in danger of spoiling. It was a flimsy excuse. Was it enough to cover her if she got caught? Did she dare try it?

Her instincts screamed at her to go have a look at that container. The combination of that spooky team of men and the strange little e-mail yesterday was too ominous to be a co-incidence. Obviously, something exceedingly sneaky was afoot. Equally obvious: if she got caught, she could be in more than trouble. But hey. She'd dedicated the past two years to becoming Danger Girl. This should be right up her alley, right?

Moving quickly before she could second-guess herself, she hunted up a clipboard while her printer spit out a quick copy of the *Zhow Min's* manifest. She grabbed it and headed out the door.

It was easier than she'd have anticipated to get onto the ship. She just strolled up the gang-plank, flashed her AbaCo ID badge, mumbled something about needing to check the paper-work on a container and the Taiwanese sailor manning the hatch shrugged and let her pass.

An interior stairway to her immediate left beckoned. She climbed it until it ran out and stepped out hesitantly onto the main cargo deck. A towering jungle of containers loomed around her. She looked to be aft of the first stack of containers, which meant she should move to the rail and follow it aft past one more stack.

In a matter of minutes, she was staring up at the green container some twenty feet over her head. Now what? She glanced left and right and spied a tall metal staircase on wheels. She moved down to it and gave it an experimental nudge. It wasn't ridiculously heavy. It took her a couple of minutes, but she managed to maneuver it into place at the base of the correct pile of containers.

She climbed it quickly. And then she made the mistake of looking down through its mesh steps and had to stop to catch her breath while a minor panic attack passed. Note to self: never look down through see-through steps. She fixed her gaze on the green box above and forced herself to keep going. *Danger Girl. I'm Danger Girl.*

She arrived at the container. It looked no different than any other reefer container around it. She inspected the door. A heavy steel bar would have to lift clear of a latch, but then it looked as though it would open. She reached for the handle. Holy crow, the thing was heavy. She heaved on it with both hands, pushing with all her might. Thighs and back straining, she managed to pop the bar free with a loud clang.

She froze. Looked left and right in panic.

Counted to a hundred, but nobody came along to check on her. She tugged on the door. Soundlessly, it opened a few inches. A strong odor of fish poured out on a gust of cold air. Starting to feel supremely foolish, she stepped into the dark space. She should've brought a flashlight. Too late to go back and fetch one now, though. She left the door cracked open and eased forward into the crowded space.

As advertised, boxes labeled salmon and caviar on ice were stacked on the left. The entire right side of the container was taken up with two massive steel containers. She lifted the lid of the first one and saw black water. Something alive squirmed a foot or so below the surface and she recoiled in horror before she remembered the live lobsters that were supposed to be in there.

So why had a team of men broken in here under cover of darkness and left backpacks of…something…behind? She kept an eye out for the black backpacks but saw no sign of them or their possible contents. As advertised, this crate seemed to contain nothing more menacing than a bunch of seafood.

She moved deeper into the crate, following a narrow aisle left open down the middle of the space. That seemed a little weird. The whole idea was to pack these things tight and not waste an inch of packing volume. These containers were not cheap to move around the world and nobody gratuitously wasted space in one.

She followed the passage deeper into the dark.

Abruptly, she came up short against a wall. And frowned. She'd thought she had another eight or ten feet to go before she reached the back wall of the container. Usually, her spatial orientation was more accurate than this. Something else was strange, too. The rows of stacked boxes stopped a good four feet from the wall, leaving a substantial gap back here. Now, that was plain wrong. No client in their right mind would load cargo this far short of the back of the box. She looked around for the contents of the missing backpacks, on the assumption that this was the spot the men must have left their loads.

Nada. The space was frustratingly empty, completely clear of anything at all. Just floors and walls back here.

She examined the exposed wall before her. It was finished with cheap paneling instead of the quilted insulation lining all of the other interior wall surfaces of this container. Indeed, all reefer units were heavily insulated to hold in cooled or heated air. Squinting to make out more detail on this oddly paneled wall, she was startled to spot some sort of electronic device mounted on the far right-hand side of it. It was tucked way back in the dark and she could hardly make it out.

She moved over to what turned out to be a numeric keypad of some kind. Her pulse leaped. This little gizmo was definitely *not* standard issue in a reefer.

As her eyes continued to adjust to the dark, the number pad glowed faintly before her. AbaCo used similar devices as locks on office doors and storage areas. Could this be a door panel of some kind? How could it not be? She was dead sure she hadn't reached the back of the container yet. There had to be a secret compartment behind the wall.

She stepped up to the pad. She couldn't very well start punching in random numbers.

Random numbers…

Could it be? She reached up and typed in the numbers that had ended yesterday's cryptic e-mail message—1-5-4-7-2. And stared in shock as a green light illuminated over the pad. A distinct clicking noise was audible. She looked for a handle but found none. Tentatively, she ran her fingertips over the paneled wall. And discovered a groove running the length of it next to the side wall of the container. She wedged her fingernails under it and gave a tug. A concealed door swung open before her.

She stepped through, terrified of what she might find. It was really dark in the closet-sized space. Only a tiny pinprick of light illuminated the far corner at floor level.

Something moved.

Something big.

She jolted violently and muffled a scream.

The thing moved again. She backed away in horror, banging into the door at her back and shoving it wide open in her haste to escape the monster lurking in the dark.

A shaft of dim light spilled into the space, vaguely illuminating the creature crouching in the corner.

Emily froze. And stared. A cold chill rippled through her and her jaw dropped in shock.

Chapter 5

Jagger lurched as steel rattled nearby. What was this? They'd fed him and given him several jugs of water last night. Nobody was scheduled to bother him for at least a week. He'd long ago figured out he was being held in some sort of shipping container. The faint but unmistakable roll of a ship and the smell of seawater gave it away. His guess was that he'd been on a ship for most of the past two years, held in international waters, tucked away and forgotten except for those times when someone came into his ten-by-ten-foot world and tried to beat or torture some more information out of him.

The first few weeks had been the worst. His

captors had been making a concerted effort to break him then, to squeeze him for everything they could get out of him while his intelligence and information were freshest. But the interrogations and beatings had tailed off over time. He suspected his captors were just waiting now for him to crack up or kill himself, whichever came first.

Except he was just too damned stubborn to give in. He'd been played for a fool, and he had no intention of going out like that. He owed his captors. Big time. And he wasn't about to die until he gave them a dose of their own medicine right back. His need for vengeance—he'd long ago quit sugarcoating his fury with words like *justice* and *payback*—had sustained him for nearly two years. In occasional moments of stark honesty, he wondered how much longer he could hang on to it. When even his hate deserted him, he feared he would be done for.

He scrabbled to the back of his box as the distinctive beep of his cage's lock sounded on the other side of the wall. They would hit him with a Taser if he was anywhere near the door when it opened. A slash of light fell on the floor. Someone slipped through the narrow gap. Odd. They usually came in threes and fours. They'd learned the hard way not to tangle with him one-on-one. In fact, they'd only made that mistake once.

Had they made it again?

He coiled, ready to spring at his captor.

The guard moved suddenly, jumping backward sharply, banging into the door. He stared, bemused as the door swung wide open. What was up with that?

A gasp. And then a voice straight out of his most painful dreams gasped, "Jagger? Is that you?"

Bright lights exploded inside his head, ice picks of shock stabbing at his eyeballs as recognition ripped through him. *What in the hell is she doing here?*

What new game were they playing with him? To date, their efforts hadn't been this sophisticated. Had Emily been dragged here to seduce him? Were they blackmailing her, perhaps? Forcing her to tease and tantalize him into spilling his guts? If brute force wouldn't work, were they now going to resort to sex? He had to admit, it was a diabolical tactic. The sort of thing he might have thought of if he were the captor and not the captive.

Surely they knew how he felt about this woman. Was a team of men waiting in the wings to swoop in and drag them apart as soon as she extracted whatever information she'd been sent here to get? He squinted past her, but it was too dark in the area beyond to see how many men waited in the shadows for him.

"Jagger?" she repeated in horror.

He must look like death warmed over. Two years with no sunlight, malnourished, unshaven. Hell, even he could barely stand his own stink.

"Emily Grainger," he muttered. "Can't say I was expecting you to walk through that door, darlin'."

"What are you doing here?" she gasped.

He laughed, and even he could hear the manic edge to it. "That's funny, Em. What do you think I'm doing here? Enjoying the soli-tude and sea breezes?"

"What are you talking about?" she de-manded, her voice barely a whisper. "Who did this to you?"

"Your cronies at AbaCo. Tossed me in this box two years ago and left me to rot."

"Two—what—how—" she sputtered. "I don't understand."

"Look. Whatever game your bosses are play-ing, you can just forget it. I'm not breaking. Get out of here and leave me alone. I'm not let-ting them sucker me into talking, even if they dangle you as bait. I'd rather have them just beat the tar out of me."

"Beat you?" A long pause. "Are you being held *prisoner?*" The last word was exhaled in a shock so profound it barely had sound. Was she really that naive? Was it just dawning on her what AbaCo was truly capable of? What did she think had happened to him two years ago when he just vanished off the face of the earth?

He replied sarcastically, "And I suppose you're here to pull off a miraculous rescue and raise my hopes that I'm actually gonna get out of here before your goon bosses grab me again. Is that what they told you to do?"

"Rescue?" She seemed to struggle to comprehend the word. "Jagger, I got an anonymous e-mail yesterday with nothing but the name of this ship and the location of this cargo container in the message. I came to check it out. I had no idea—" She broke off. "We have to get you out of here!"

"Riiiight," he drawled.

"I'm serious. Come on! My boss will only be in his meeting a little while longer. If anyone on this island is responsible for holding you prisoner, he's the one." When he didn't move, she added urgently, "Come. *On.*"

He couldn't help it. In spite of himself, a flicker of hope ignited in his gut. Dammit, he shouldn't play along with this new ploy of theirs. He knew better. But maybe, just maybe, there was a chance they would screw something up. That he could actually slip past his captors and win his freedom for real. It was absolutely a trap. But a trap could work two ways.

Of course, he might die in the attempt. But at this point, death held very little intimidation value for him. He almost wished for it sometimes.

He eased to his feet. Took a step forward. She backed up, shoving the door behind her open wider. The smell of fish grew even stronger than usual. He was never going to eat seafood again if he made it out of here.

Emily turned and disappeared from sight down a narrow gap between floor-to-ceiling wooden packing crates.

He took another step forward. *Out of the box.* Mother of God, he was out of that box. Even if it was only for a few more seconds, it was worth whatever they did to him to have made it out of that crate alive. Frowning, he pushed the door closed behind him. It clicked shut and a tiny red light illuminated over the electronic lock. If he was actually expecting to make it out of here, he'd cover his tracks and make it look as if he were still safely locked up inside his tiny prison.

Frankly, he was stunned that a team of AbaCo's men wasn't out here waiting for him, laughing their heads off at his pitiful hope that he'd actually been rescued. But the box seemed tightly packed with seafood, and if there were any hiding spots from which his captors were planning to jump out at him, he sure couldn't see them.

The flicker of hope in his gut grew a little stronger.

Cautiously, he made his way down the aisle, squinting as blinding light assaulted his eyes. His eyeballs ached almost unbearably from it. Nonetheless he was grateful for the pain because it meant he could still see normally.

Emily paused short of the door at the far end of the box.

He asked, "How do you plan to get out of here with me? Just walk out?"

She frowned. "Have you got any better ideas? You can't exactly jump overboard. It's too far to fall without killing yourself when you hit the water, and besides, someone would hear you."

He stepped into the doorway and reeled back, unprepared to be twenty feet or more above the deck with only a flimsy, metal mesh staircase between him and a nasty fall.

Emily continued, "The men who came in here last night came aboard using ropes. They climbed up the side of the ship and went back down the same way."

"You *saw* them?" He didn't associate Aba-Co's people with being so careless.

"Well, I wasn't supposed to. But I couldn't sleep and I happened to be out for a walk when the *Zhow Min* docked, and I happened to be standing at the right angle to see the silhouettes of the men climbing the hull."

"Do they know you saw them?"

"I don't think so. They had a lookout posted and he didn't seem alarmed by anything. Only problem is that just as I was leaving the area, my boss found me."

"Was he suspicious?" Jagger asked quickly.

"He's always suspicious. But I think he

bought my story about not being able to sleep after the big meal the company served at the party."

Party. Right. New Year's Eve. His gut twisted violently at the reminder of the import of that particular date in his life. Except, if this little escape attempt of Emily's, which supposedly had been prompted by events on this New Year's Eve, turned into real freedom for him, he might have to revise his currently low opinion of the holiday.

Speaking of escaping, he looked around quickly. "We need to get moving. If I had a rope, I could climb down the hull, too."

She started down the stairs, whispering over her shoulder, "Maybe I can find you one. Stay here while I go have a look."

Right. As if he was waiting around for the goon squad to close in on them. Not a chance. He hurried down the steps on her heels. Interestingly enough, she made no comment. She headed to her left and he spied a deck railing not far ahead of her. She leaned out over the side of the ship, looking in both directions, then hurried back to him where he lurked in the shadow of a giant pile of shipping containers.

"There's a rope hanging almost all the way down to the dock about fifty feet to your right as you reach the railing. You can't exactly stroll down the dock barefoot and looking like a mountain man, though. Somebody'd spot you for sure."

No lie. He eased forward, sticking to the shadows as much as possible, until he could lean far enough forward to peek over the railing at the pier below. It wasn't busy, but neither was it deserted.

"Do you know if the pier is hollow or maybe constructed of wood? Can I get beneath it?" he asked under his breath.

"I think so. But you'll have to be careful. AbaCo has divers in the water to make sure no one sabotages a ship while it's here."

He blinked in surprise. She probably shouldn't have told him that if she was supposed to be protecting AbaCo's security.

She continued rapidly, "This island is about

one mile in diameter. On the far side of it from here is a little beach. It's surrounded by thick underbrush. If you can make it over there, you can hide in that area. Unfortunately, most of the rest of the island is bare rocks. I'll have to wait until tonight, but I ought to be able to bring you fresh clothes and supplies at the beach. And then we can figure out what we're doing from there."

"This is an island?" he asked sharply. "Where are we?"

"They call it the Rock. It's a private island at the far western end of the Hawaiian island chain."

He swore under his breath. No wonder Aba-Co's guys were in no hurry to close in on him. They knew he couldn't go anywhere. "How do people get on and off the island?" he asked.

Emily answered, "Boats, mostly. Sometimes helicopters. They head over to Lokaina, which is the nearest permanently settled island, and fly from the airport there to the bigger islands. It's almost twenty miles from here."

He thought fast. "Can you get us a boat?" It

was the only realistic option for him. No way could he swim twenty miles of open ocean. He wasn't that fit. Heck, Navy SEALs were hardly that fit.

But if he could snag a boat, twenty miles wasn't far at all. An hour, maybe. And an airport on Lokaina? That he could work with. If he could just make it over there, he might stand a real chance of getting free of his captors. As soon as he contacted his superiors they'd send in whatever forces it took to retrieve him.

"Can cell phones call off this island?"

She shook her head. "Only satellite phones, and they're pretty expensive. The office has sat lines that everyone's allowed to use."

Yeah, and AbaCo was sure to monitor every last one of them. Yup, he'd have to get his butt over to Lokaina before he could call in the cavalry.

Damn. This was starting to feel like a real escape. Of course, his captors were probably getting a kick out of giving him a few hours of illusory freedom like this. No doubt they planned to close in on him at this supposed rendezvous tonight and take him down then. Or at least they'd try.

But then, he wasn't entirely incapable of throwing them a few surprises of his own.

He grabbed the thick nylon line and swung his foot over the railing. "When will you come to the beach?" he asked.

"An hour after dark?" she replied questioningly.

He nodded. "Done. I'll see you there."

To say she was shell-shocked was a bit of an understatement. Emily stumbled off the *Zhow Min* in a fog, barely aware of having closed the reefer unit's outer door and pushing the stairs back to where she'd gotten them.

Jagger had been held prisoner all this time? Incredible. Worse, he believed AbaCo was behind his kidnapping. Unfortunately, in her heart of hearts, she believed that AbaCo was absolutely capable of doing such a thing. She should have left the company a long time ago. But the money and benefits were excellent, and she'd preferred to be safe and secure in that steady paycheck.

Some Danger Girl she'd turned out to be. She'd continued to work for the evil supervillains, even after she strongly suspected they were up to no good. She'd let her wallet rule her ethics.

Thank God MysteryMom had sent that e-mail to her. Even if she'd had no idea what it meant, it had made her edgy and sleepless enough to see those men climb aboard the ship last night. Without that, she'd never have found him.

Nausea rumbled through her gut at what would have happened to him had she not investigated that broken-into reefer unit. Would he have died in that box? How could he not have? It wasn't as if AbaCo could turn him loose to press charges against them and testify about his captivity.

She glanced down at her watch and gasped in dismay. Schroder's meeting was due to end in a few minutes and he was super punctual.

Crud. She picked up her pace until she was all but running.

She slipped into her desk chair, hot and sticky, her hair flying every which way, about two minutes before Schroder and his cronies emerged from their meeting, laughing. She managed to compose her facial expression, but her heart still pounded in fear at the sight of him. She reached for her in-basket and knocked over a coffee mug in her haste. Blessedly, it was empty, but Shroder looked up at the thud. She smiled lamely, her face red, and with exaggerated care, righted the cup.

The afternoon seemed to last about a week, but finally, the clock said five o'clock. All her work was done, and she shut down her computer quickly. She was surprised to notice that her hands were shaking. She had to get a grip on herself if she was going to be of the slightest use to Jagger.

She made her way back to the staff dormitory where the employees all had their own small room on the island. It allowed folks to permanently store clothing and toiletries and not have to move personal possessions back and forth to the Rock when it was their turn to work. It kept hauling luggage out here down to a minimum, and she supposed that saved the company money on top of being convenient for the workers.

Her plan this evening was to break into the room next to hers, which was held by a guy currently not on the island, and borrow some clothes for Jagger. The two men were reasonably close in height and build. Her room shared a kitchenette with her coworker's and only a simple lock held the door to his room shut.

It only took about fifteen seconds and an ice pick to pop the lock into the guy's quarters. It was disconcerting to realize just how insecure she'd been all this time on the island. She stepped into the dim room and made her way to his closet. Slacks, a golf shirt, shoes, socks and underwear went into her waterproof canvas beach bag. She glimpsed the bathroom behind a partially open door and swung in there for a razor, nail clippers and a comb. She hit the jackpot when she spied a new toothbrush still in its wrapper. She grabbed it and some dental floss while she was at it.

In her own room, she added bottled water, snacks, a small first aid kit, a pocketknife and a flashlight to her bag of goodies. Last, she picked up the coup de grace. During Schroder's afternoon coffee break, she'd managed to lift a spare set of keys to the island's small runabout boat from a drawer in his desk.

Twilight had settled over the island but it wasn't dark yet. She gulped down something tasteless out of the microwave and stared anxiously at the clock beside her bed. Her mind was blank, filled only with terror that she was going to screw this up and get Jagger hurt or worse. Danger Girl must not fail!

When she judged an hour had passed since full darkness had fallen, she put on her running shoes, picked up her bag and headed out. Here went nothing.

The beach bag converted to a mini-backpack, so she slung it over her shoulders and took off jogging down the trail that followed the coast all the way around the island. She prayed she could keep up a credible pace until she topped the ridge and disappeared from sight of the clustered buildings.

The rocks rose behind her and hid her from sight. She slowed, panting. Lord, she hated running. She walked carefully as her eyes slowly adjusted to the dim conditions. Although the trail was mostly smooth, washes of loose sand and gravel made it treacherous in spots. It descended the far side of the island's spine in a series of sharp switchbacks that wound toward the eastern shore, but as she approached the lee side of the island, it leveled out. She watched carefully for the turnoff that led to the beach where she said she'd meet Jagger.

There. In the shadow of a koa tree. The faint white stripe of a trail. She turned down it, ducking into the lush undergrowth. This little corner of the island, protected from the worst of the trade winds, was thick with native Hawaiian plant life.

The tiny beach came into view. Maybe only fifty feet long, it was tucked between a pair of giant volcanic boulders at each end. Foot-high waves lapped quietly onto the sand, funneled up the beach by the outcroppings at each end of the inlet.

There was no sign of Jagger. Had he been caught? Panic turned her knees to jelly. Now what was she supposed to do? It would take hours for any police to arrive on the Rock, assuming they would even respond to an outrageous claim of a man held hostage for two years in a cargo container. Besides, Schroder and his men could have Jagger off the island and spirited away into a new and even more obscure captivity long before the police could get here.

"Jagger?" she called out quietly. "It's me."

Nothing.

She frowned. Maybe he'd already found some other way off the island. In which case, she'd wait here for a while, figure out she'd been stood up and return to her room. And then what should she do? Let him disappear again from her life? Spend the next two years wondering if he was AbaCo's captive or worse?

Knowing what she knew now, how would she survive that?

Losing him the first time had been more painful than she could've imagined. They'd formed such a close bond so quickly, had clicked so well, that when he ditched her she'd been utterly devastated. She never had actually gotten over him or moved past him. But then, how could she? She saw his face every day. Couldn't help but think of him every day. Heck, she'd transformed herself into Danger Girl to be the kind of woman he'd be attracted to. It was as if that one magical night had taken over her life, as if it had never really ended. The whole past two years had been about Jagger.

And if she had to go forward again into another endless abyss of unanswered questions, of self-doubt, of missing him, she didn't know if she could take it.

Of course, the whole blessed thing was out of her hands. He would either keep their appointment here or he wouldn't. She hated being powerless like this! *C'mon, Jagger. Show up.*

* * *

Jagger crouched in a crevice high in the rock outcropping that bounded the south end of the tiny beach. Emily was sitting in the sand, jumping a mile high at every little night sound. He hadn't spotted the trap yet, which worried him. Enough for him to continue holding his position here while he waited for AbaCo's goons to show themselves. From time to time Emily glanced at her watch, but she gave no other visible signal to anyone who might be lurking nearby, watching her.

An hour passed. She was growing more agitated and jumpy by the minute. Still no sign of the ambush, though. Was it possible that she'd been telling the truth earlier? That she wasn't in league with his captors, willingly or otherwise? He dismissed the idea as preposterous. How could she not be doing their dirty work? She was out here on this godforsaken island earning a paycheck from AbaCo, wasn't she?

Her shoulders began to droop. If he wasn't mistaken, she wiped away tears from her cheeks at one point. The stress must be getting to her. It was getting to him, too. Had he not spent the past two years sitting in a box, he'd have been squirming hard an hour ago. He had to give these AbaCo guys credit. They were patient.

His attention jerked back to Emily as she stood up with an audible sigh. His gaze narrowed as she made her way over to the outcropping practically at his feet. She put down a dark bag, wedging it into a crack at the base of the boulder and murmured, "Godspeed, wherever you are tonight, Jagger."

As she trudged up the beach with her back to him, he hopped down silently and picked up the bag. He pulled the drawstring open and peered in at the contents. Something cracked painfully in his chest and his next breath was hard to draw. He stared down at the clothing, food and toiletries, flummoxed. What was she up to?

He glanced up and she was just disappearing into the trees. Still no movement whatsoever. No sign of an ambush anywhere. He should turn around and leave. Take the peace offering without looking back and use the gear and clothing to get off this rock.

But instead, he ran lightly across the beach and darted into the woods, parallel to the path, ducking from shadow to shadow. As hard as he found it to believe, he was forced to conclude that there was no one else out here.

Still, it was sheer insanity to call out low, "Emily. Wait up." But call he did.

She whirled, peering into the trees, trying to spot him. He held his position cautiously, his eyes roving urgently, looking for other reactions to his voice. Nada.

"Go back to the beach," he murmured.

She complied instantly, all but running back toward the strip of sand. He turned slowly to follow. Either there was more to this situation than he was seeing or he was the biggest idiot in the universe to fall for the same trap, baited by the same woman, twice.

There was only one way to find out for sure. And apparently he was going to do that one thing, since his feet were already carrying him back to the beach and whatever awaited him there.

Chapter 6

Emily's heart lodged in her throat at that husky, familiar voice caressing her skin out of the darkness. Memories long repressed surged back into her consciousness. Sweat-slicked skin on skin, his hard power driving into her, her body arching up into that mind-blowing pleasure, all her fantasies and more come to life.

She stopped at the edge of the minijungle, waiting for him to join her, huffing from the quick hike. Yeah, that was the reason she was panting. The hike.

Only the waves and the wind in the palm fronds overhead broke the night's sultry silence. But then something hard slapped over her mouth and she about jumped out of her skin. Heat caressed her ear—oh, God, his mouth—and he whispered, "Don't move. Don't make a sound."

She nodded her head fractionally beneath his hard hand. The unrelenting pressure eased slowly. Had he not told her to be still she'd have turned in his arms and flung herself at him in her relief. She stood there for a long time, his presence druggingly close and emanating heat and sex, but never, not once, touching her after his hand fell away from her. It was maddening.

Finally, an eternity later, he murmured, "What's in the bag?"

Her gaze snapped over to the beach bag still sitting at the base of the boulders across the beach. He'd seen that, huh? Then why hadn't he shown himself earlier? *Ah.* It hit her. He'd been waiting to see if it was some kind of trap. She answered, "Clothes. Food. Supplies."

He nodded, almost as if she'd passed some sort of test. Then he muttered, "I need to get off this island before I'm discovered missing."

She replied lightly, "Ya think? By the way, can I move now?"

His low chuckle stirred her hair and her heart. "You know the drill, Danger Girl. Hold your hands well away from your body and no sudden moves."

He remembers Danger Girl. What other details of that one night together did he remember? Then his terse instructions registered. "Sheesh, Jagger. I'm not a criminal. I'm helping you, for crying out loud."

"It's not you I'm worried about," he responded. "I can take you. But a half dozen of your partners in crime? Not so much."

He could take her? He undoubtedly meant that as in to take her down in a fight, but the images his double entendre sent spiraling through her mind stole her breath away. Dang it, where had her knees disappeared to all of a sudden? They'd gone squishy and would hardly bear her weight.

She whispered, "There's no one else out here as far as I know."

The sound he made in response was skeptical. Appalled, she looked at the surrounding undergrowth, peering fearfully into it in search of bogeymen and bad guys. She hadn't seen anyone follow her out here, and she'd looked over her shoulder constantly on the hike across the island.

If she didn't understand that he'd been through a horrendous ordeal and wasn't yet clear from danger, she'd be hurt by his lack of faith in her. But as it was, she fully understood his caution. She only prayed he was wrong.

Her scan brought her gaze around full circle back to him. Even in the moonlight his face looked paler than it should be. So thin he was. As if all of his excess being had been pared away until only the essentials remained. His was the physique of a man who'd survived immense suffering.

"I know how we can get you off the island," she offered.

"Do tell."

"I borrowed the spare keys to a boat this afternoon."

"One of the cigarettes?" he asked hopefully.

"No such luck. It's a twenty-two-foot ski boat that the staff uses for recreation—snorkeling and diving and some water-skiing when the seas are calm. But it'll take us to Lokaina."

"And where are these keys?" he asked intently.

"In my right pants pocket."

She started to reach for them, but he lurched violently and leaped forward to stop her movement, gripping her wrist in a vise that all but crushed her bones.

"I'll get them," he bit out.

Man. Touchy, touchy. But then his big hand slid into her pocket, only a thin layer of cotton separating his fingers from her groin, and her brain froze. Or maybe *overheated* was a better description. Her body went hot and liquid and achy all of its own volition, and suddenly her spine felt completely unhinged.

"While I've got my hands on you, I may as well go ahead and search you. I'll have to do it sooner or later anyway."

She blinked at his muttered words. He didn't sound particularly thrilled at the prospect, and disappointment coursed through her. Was touching her like this doing nothing at all to him? Her pulse was far too thrilled for its own good at the prospect of having his hands roam all over her body once more. He took a step forward, looming in front of her, so close she could count his eyelashes.

And then his hands touched her ribs underneath her T-shirt. Her breathing hitched, suspended somewhere between a gasp and a groan. His palms skimmed up the sides of her breasts, across the ticklishness of her armpits, tracing her collarbones and then swooping down between her breasts. His hands spread apart then, cupping her breasts. Surely through the thin lace of her bra he could feel that she wore no surveillance wire. Of course, just as surely he could feel the way her nipples had pebbled up hard and eager in response to his touch.

Her face flamed. Not because she was embarrassed. Oh, no. It was far more humiliating than that. She was aroused. By a man who'd blatantly seduced her, and then disappeared from her life for long enough that she should've been *way* over him by now. By a man who made outrageous claims about being a prisoner in a box for the past two years and had some evidence to support him. By a man she barely knew and yet of whom her memories were mostly naked and intensely sexual.

One of his hands emerged from under her shirt to spear into the hair at the back of her neck while the other hand slid around to her back. Hard, hot fingers trailed down her spine, dipping into the crevice as the base of her spine possessively. She arched forward reflexively, away from the intimate invasion, and her hips ran squarely—and informatively—into his groin.

Well, then. He wasn't completely unaffected by this search, either. Did it mean anything at all? Or was it purely a function of him not having touched a woman in two years? Whereas she could hardly stay on her feet as lust slammed into her, he merely shot her a shark's grin that gleamed briefly in the dark. Clearly, he was enjoying torturing Danger Girl.

If only she had the same power over him. Then the contest might be a little more even.

A quickly as he'd commenced the search, it was over. His hands withdrew, leaving her shivering and bereft. His voice, as calm as a glassy sea, flowed over her. "Okay. So we've ruled out a wire. Do you have a burr or some other tracking device on you? Will you tell me the truth or do I need to strip you naked and dunk all of your clothes in the ocean?"

Hmm. He could always have left her clothes on her and told her to swim out into the water a ways. But no. Getting her naked was on his mind, instead. Maybe the contest between Danger Girl and the Super Spy wasn't quite so uneven after all.

She answered him earnestly, "I'm not wearing a radio or tracking device or anything else like that. I give you my word."

He stared at her for a long moment. "I shouldn't believe you," he mumbled under his breath. "I know better."

She frowned. What was he talking about? He'd commented earlier something to the effect of her helping AbaCo set him up. Of course, that was sheer lunacy. She would never have done such a thing, particularly not to him. Not a man she'd been wildly infatuated with and had even bedded. Heck, one with whom she was still wildly infatuated.

"Where's this boat of yours?" he asked abruptly.

"That way." She pointed off to her right. "At the employee dock. It's tied up with the two cigarette boats and some Jet Skis, but I don't have the keys to any of those."

"Is this dock guarded?"

"From who? Everyone here works for AbaCo."

"Perfect," he purred. "Let's go."

Apparently, he was expecting her to assist in the next bit of grand larceny. She frowned. "I can't go with you."

"Yeah, you can—and are," he retorted.

"But I've got responsibilities. I need this job."

"Do you need to be dead also?" he snapped.

"I'm serious, Jagger. I don't mind helping you escape, but I can't up and leave. I'm not that carefree bachelorette you met two years ago."

He snorted. "And when they discover my crate's empty, what exactly do you think they'll do?"

"I don't know."

"I'll tell you, Emily. They'll pull the surveillance tapes from the dock and spot you going aboard the ship. They'll go through the ship's security camera logs and find you going into that container and both of us coming out of it. And then they'll come after you. Not to fire you. To kill you."

She gaped at him, too horrified to say a word.

"Come on. You're leaving tonight. With me."

Stunned, she didn't argue as he dragged her forward by the hand toward the black bag of supplies and then off toward the boat dock. What he said was logical. It just refused to compute. Someone would try to kill her? Not possible. She was a regular person living a reasonably regular life—even if her job was in an exotic locale. It was still mostly pushing paper at a desk. Danger Girl was about making adventurous choices, not fighting supervillains and risking death!

Jagger dragged her along for several silent and scary minutes. Then without warning he dropped to a crouch and yanked her down beside him. "That the dock?" he breathed.

She looked ahead and saw the small pier jutting out into the ocean. "Yes. That's it."

He watched it for several nerve-racking minutes and then announced, "It looks clear. Here's what you're going to do. Walk down to the dock and untie the boat. Don't get in it and don't start the engine if there happens to be a key in the ignition. You and I are going to tow the boat clear of the dock and out into open water before we crank her up. Otherwise we risk drawing someone's attention."

"How are we going to tow it—"

He cut her off. "Just go untie the boat. And wait for me if I'm not there before you." Before she could ask any more questions, he darted off down the beach toward the boathouse and was gone. How were they going to tow a boat? Why couldn't she start the boat if there was already a key? Did he think it would blow up or something? And most important of all, how was she supposed to inform him that she wasn't this kind of Danger Girl at all? That she was actually Giant Chicken Girl when it came to doing anything that involved adrenaline or death?

If he was right, it would be more dangerous for her to stay here on the island than it would be for her to march down there and steal a boat. That one fact alone was the sole reason she stood up and forced her feet into motion.

Her skin crawled with the nakedness of standing out here on the rocks like this. She tried reminding herself that she had every right to be here and her presence shouldn't raise any but the mildest suspicions in anyone's mind if she was spotted. It didn't help. Danger Girl was officially retired. Trembling, she stumbled forward and nearly pitched face-first onto the volcanic rock. She righted herself at the last moment and stood still, panting, until she caught her breath.

Darn it, she could do this. She'd rescued Jagger and that had been way more scary than this. Besides, whether he admitted it or not, he needed her help. He was by no means operating at full strength physically, and probably not mentally or emotionally, either.

Doggedly, she pressed on. She fixed her gaze on the wooden dock and strode down to it, gazing neither left nor right as she approached it. If someone was out here watching her, so be it. There wasn't a thing she could do about it. She would just have to claim sleepwalking or a sudden urge for a moonlit cruise around the island. Neither one would fly with Schroder—he was far too clever for that—but the excuse would have to suffice. It was all she had. That and a burning need to be with the man who'd stolen her heart and never given it back.

As grim thoughts of what Schroder would do to her if he caught her flitted through her mind, she made her way out the narrow pier to the ski boat. Two lines moored the craft. Despite her shaking hands, she managed to unleash the boat from its hitching post. Now what? Jagger had told her to stay put until he joined her. What did that mean? She risked a look back toward shore and saw no sign of his familiar silhouette approaching.

And then a voice whispered from practically under her feet, "Push the boat back. Then sit down on the dock and slide into the water."

What? She stared down in shock.

"Move."

She lurched into motion at Jagger's sharp order, doing as he said. Until her feet dangled over the water, that is. "I'll get my clothes all wet," she complained under her breath.

A snort rumbled out of the darkness. "And that's so much more important than getting shot, after all."

She sighed and eased off the pier into the Pacific Ocean. The water was nearly up to her chin here, and when a wave came in, her feet lifted briefly off the seabed.

"Grab this tow line," Jagger murmured. "I've made a loop in it. Put it under your armpits and that'll free up your arms to swim."

She did as he suggested while he rigged another line in similar fashion for himself. It was slow going pulling the boat out of the tiny marina. They reached the end of the dock and Jagger made to turn left. But then inspiration hit her.

"Go right," she urged. "There's a riptide beyond the marina, just past those rocks over there. AbaCo doesn't allow any swimming in that spot because of it."

He frowned. "That way takes us back toward the buildings."

She argued, "Once the tide catches us, it'll pull us out to sea about a hundred times faster than you and I can swim against the surf to tug this monster offshore."

He considered briefly. Then said decisively, "Okay. Let's go get your riptide."

It turned out to be surprisingly easy. One minute they were swimming laboriously, getting nowhere fast, and the next, the boat was floating out to sea so quickly it was tugging them along in its wake. Jagger had to help her make her way hand over hand up the rope toward the boat, in fact. He crawled in first and lowered a ladder over the side for her to scramble up. They drifted for a few more minutes.

The riptide petered out about a half mile from shore. As the boat slowed and began to drift south, Jagger started the engine. He left the running lights and instrument lights off, however, as he turned the craft east, and the Rock retreated to a speck in the distance.

Jagger opened up the throttles, checked the dashboard-mounted compass and made a minor course correction. The craft could make a steady twenty knots, but the sea was choppy enough tonight that he backed off to more like fifteen. At this rate, it should take them a little over an hour to reach Lokaina.

He kept glancing back over his shoulder behind them. It took her several times looking back herself to realize what he was doing. He was watching for pursuit. She thought of the sleek cigarette boats back at the dock and suddenly her exhilaration at being out here with the wind in her hair and the sea spray on her skin morphed into cold, damp terror.

But as the miles passed and the sea remained a featureless black sheet behind them, she began to breathe more normally.

They'd been on the water an hour when Jagger shouted suddenly over the motor, "Are there binoculars on this tub?"

She indicated that she didn't know but would have a look. She opened up one of the storage chests under a seat in the back of the boat and fished around. Life jackets, flares and coiled ropes. She shifted over to the other storage chest. This one held a variety of small tools and gadgets…and a nice pair of Zeiss binoculars. She grabbed them and headed back to the cockpit.

"Here ya go."

"Thanks." He took them and scanned the horizon, first behind them, then in front of them. With a low exclamation of pleasure, he turned the boat to the northeast and pushed the throttles forward. She looked in that direction. She couldn't be sure, but that might be a twinkle of lights low on the horizon.

A few more minutes confirmed her suspicion. A line of lights was visible, and before long, the black hump of an island. Lokaina. They'd made it.

Relief soared through her and she grinned over at Jagger.

And then he frowned. Lifted the binoculars again and scanned carefully behind them. He swore under his breath. He pushed the throttles all the way to the forward stop and the boat leaped over the waves, jarring her in her seat.

"Take the wheel," he bit out grimly.

She slid over into his seat as he stood up and moved aside. "What's up?" she shouted.

"We're about to have company."

Chapter 7

Emily's heart dropped to her feet. She looked back over her shoulder but could see nothing through the rooster tail of spray. Not that she needed to. She knew exactly what was back there. A big, black, lethal boat bearing down upon them. Fast.

Jagger tossed her a life jacket with a terse command to put it on as he fished out what looked like a waterproof bag. He tied it around his waist with one of the ropes from the equipment chest. Quickly, he stuffed the entire knapsack she'd brought for him into the bag and sealed it shut.

He put his mouth close to her ear and shouted, "I'll get us as close to shore as I can.

They're probably going to shoot at us. When I tell you to, dive overboard. Stay underwater as long as you can. When you come up, only come up enough to get some air and then go back down. When you can't hear their boat anymore, surface and swim for shore. It may take a while for them to leave the area, so be prepared to bob in the water for a while. Got it?"

She nodded, too terrified to do anything else.

He continued, "It's me they're after. Just get away from me as fast as you can and you should be safe enough."

Horror flowed through her. "I'm not leaving you!"

Jagger scowled. "You don't have to pretend to be a hero for me. I know the score. You drew me out, now they'll finish me off. No hard feelings, babe. Dying like this is a hell of a lot better than spending another day in that damned crate. I knew what I was walking into when I left that box with you."

"What are you talking about?" she demanded.

He frowned but didn't reply. She opened her

mouth to insist on an explanation, but before she could say anything, a roar became audible behind them.

"Don't forget what I told you," he yelled. And then he was behind her, slipping into the driver's seat as she slid out of his way. He took over the wheel. "Get down!" he ordered. "Lie flat back there and stay out of sight until I tell you to jump."

The boat slapped down on the waves, jarring her teeth, but Jagger just continued to shove the throttle as far open as it would go. The boat swerved violently, first left, then right. And the roar from behind them was all around them now. Their small craft rocked violently, as if it had crossed another boat's wake at an oblique angle.

Jagger shouted, "Get ready, Emily! Jump over the port side on my command!" He must have realized she'd have no idea what port was, because he shouted again, "Jump over the side opposite me!"

That she understood. She pushed up to her hands and knees, but the way the boat was bouncing around, that was about all she could manage. She checked the straps on her life vest.

And then he shouted, "Go!"

She didn't stand up and jump so much as slither over the side of the boat on her belly and flop into the water. Except it felt more like crashing into concrete than hitting water. With an oomph, the air slammed out of her lungs and frigid blackness closed in on her. The shock of it stole away what little breath she had left.

Up. Which way was up? A moment of panic clawed at her until she stopped sinking. The life vest kicked in then, pulling her up toward the surface. She kicked and pulled with her arms. Her clothes were unbelievably heavy, even with the vest's buoyancy to help. Her lungs burned and her eyes stung ferociously as salt water hit them. A faint glimmer above caught her attention, and then she broke through to the surface. Her face felt cold air upon it and she drew in a gulping, desperate breath. One more breath, and then she remembered Jagger's instructions. She pulled in a last deep breath and bobbed under the water, using her arms to push herself down against the upward push of the life jacket.

She surfaced again, this time registering the roar of boat engines nearby. She said a quick prayer that one of them wouldn't run her over.

She'd ducked and bobbed a few more times when, as she held herself underwater, a tremendous concussion of sound and pressure slammed into her just as a bright orange flash exploded overhead. The water around her glowed with it. *Ohmigosh. What was that?*

She stayed under as long as she could, but the demands of being an air-breathing creature finally won out and she headed for the surface. The sight that greeted her made her blood run cold. Their ski boat was split in two, its halves flaming while burning oil and debris littered the surface of the ocean around it. The bastards had blown up the boat!

And Jagger? What of him?

She looked around frantically for any sign of him in the water. And realized belatedly that the fires had effectively illuminated the entire area, to include her. She took a hasty breath and ducked under again. The next two times she breathed, she barely broke the surface with her mouth and nose before heading back down. Even then, she still heard the rumble of the AbaCo boat circling the wreckage. Schroder's boys were no doubt checking to make sure they'd killed Jagger.

After an eternity, she finally surfaced to the sound of silence. Cautiously, she stayed afloat, turning in a full three-hundred-sixty-degree circle. No sign of the AbaCo boat. A swell lifted her up and she gazed around once more. There. Off to her left. The lights of Lokaina. Jagger had told her to swim for it. And it wasn't as if she could float around out here indefinitely. She started paddling.

It was slow going with the bulky life jacket on, but it allowed her to flip over on her back and rest now and then. And in those moments, it was worth its weight in gold. She hoped Jagger had one. Heck, she just hoped he was alive.

How long it took her to swim to shore was anyone's guess. Two hours, maybe. Long enough that she was dog tired and never wanted to taste seawater again in her life. But finally, she stretched out on the beach, the cold sand clammy and wonderful beneath her cheek.

Her clothes were sodden and stuck to her, but as she lay there, they gradually dried out a little. Her shoes sloshed when she stumbled to the edge of the narrow strip of sand. The airport was on this side of the island. Her wallet was still in the back pocket of her sweatpants. Which meant she had a credit card. Which meant she could hire a plane and a pilot to get her the heck out of here. She suddenly felt a burning need to get home. To her family. To safety.

She stripped off most of her clothes and draped them over bushes to drip while she dried out and warmed up a bit. Then she sat down on a boulder to figure out what she was going to do next.

Shock was her main emotion. Someone had

just tried to kill her. Or at least the person with her. Things like this didn't *happen* to people like her! And Jagger? What of him? Was he dead or alive? Floating around out there in the ocean too hurt to swim ashore, or maybe blown into tiny little pieces of shark bait? God, she hated not knowing.

Again.

The same questions that had been her constant companions for the past two years surged back, stronger than ever. Where was he? What had happened to him? Was he all right? Did he want to be with her?

She couldn't do this again. It would kill her this time, knowing what she did now. She stared out to sea, scanning the detritus of the explosion that washed ashore, watching for some sign of Jagger. An article of clothing or something, anything, to wash up onto the beach that let her know what had happened to him. She couldn't imagine losing him again like this, without any warning at all. One minute he was there, and the next he was gone. Damn her fickle heart. Why couldn't she just let go of him once and for all and be done with him?

Of course she knew the answer to that. They had a bond between them that could never be severed, for better or worse.

After a while, her thoughts began to stray. The AbaCo gig was pretty much a goner. It had been a good job while it lasted. Too bad she wouldn't be getting a recommendation from her boss. It would've helped her when she started job-hunting again. But hey, at least she was alive.

How long she sat there hugging her knees and shivering, partly in cold and partly in shock, she didn't know. The moon climbed high into the sky before she finally roused herself and picked up her clothes. Shimmying into soggy sweatpants was the pits, and her T-shirt stunk of seaweed. Yuck. But she couldn't exactly stroll into the airport in her underwear. She shoved her feet into her shoes and was leaning down to tie them when a voice from nearby startled her violently.

"Going somewhere?"

She lurched, laces forgotten. "Jagger!" She flung herself at him, wrapping her arms around his neck.

He grunted in pain and staggered, hanging on to her until he righted himself. And then he reached for her wrists and unwrapped them gently, setting her away from him.

"You okay?" he rasped.

"Just wet. You?"

"A little singed around the edges, but I'll live."

"What happened?" she asked urgently. "I saw the boat explode and you weren't in the water and I was so scared they'd killed you—"

He cut her off. "That was the idea. To make them believe they'd killed me."

"Oh." A pause. "So are we safe now?"

He snorted. "I doubt it. AbaCo is nothing if not thorough. Until they find my body, or at least parts of it, they'll keep hunting me. Speaking of which, I've got to get out of here." He glanced around tensely. "Thanks for your help."

He took a step away from her as if he was

going to leave her there. Ha! Not bloody likely she was letting him slip away from her again.

"What are you talking about?" she asked lightly. "I'm not leaving you alone for a single minute. Every time you leave my sight, something disastrous happens to you. Only way to keep you safe is for me to keep an eagle eye on you, mister."

He stared in naked surprise for a moment, but then, inexplicably, his gaze hardened. "So. The game goes on, does it? What's the next gambit?"

Huh? Half the time she didn't have the faintest idea what he was talking about. When they got somewhere safe and quiet, she was going to do whatever it took to force him to explain himself. Clearly.

In answer to his question, she said, "I have credit cards with me. We can hire a plane and get out of here."

His right eyebrow arched. "Indeed? They're really going to great trouble to make me believe I got away. What do they want from me, anyway?"

He was doing it again. Talking in riddles. She said patiently, "The airport's on this side of the island. We're probably a five-minute walk from it."

He nodded. "Let me change into dry clothes if you don't mind."

She shrugged and he stepped off into the trees for a moment. The stuff she'd filched back at the Rock didn't fit him half-bad. Of course, he'd look suave and sophisticated wearing a burlap sack.

He led the way through a bit of underbrush, and then they emerged onto a dirt road. "Left or right?" he asked.

She considered briefly. "Left, I think. But I'm not a hundred percent sure."

"Good enough for me," he murmured.

It turned out to be more like a ten-minute walk to the airport, which wasn't bad, considering. It was a whole lot better than swimming forever. She pointed out the charter service that AbaCo used, and whose owner she knew fairly well. She told Jagger the guy might do her a favor if she asked him nicely.

Jagger led the way into the tiny office, which she was surprised was even open at this time of night. It must be pushing midnight.

Don Pinkerton, the owner of the island's lone charter aviation business, emerged from a back room when they walked in the front door of his place. A television muttered in the background. He peered at her in disbelief. She must look like a drowned rat.

"Emily Grainger? Is that you?"

"Hi, Don." She gave him her best smile. He flew most of the AbaCo employees back and forth between here and the other Hawaiian islands, and in the past two years, she'd developed a passing acquaintance with him. He'd flirted with her enough to signal that he'd be willing to turn their friendship into more, but she'd never taken him up on it. Her personal life was complicated enough without adding him to the mix.

"What brings you here at this hour…and soaked to the skin?"

She looked down at herself and laughed ruefully. "Long story. I have a huge favor to ask of you. My friend and I need to get out of here as soon as possible. When's the first flight?"

"Where y'all headed?" Don asked around the toothpick hanging precariously in the corner of his mouth. "Going home to Kauai?"

"Uh, ye—"

Jagger cut her off. "Actually, we could use a lift to the big island. I have to get stateside ASAP."

Don shrugged. "How big a hurry are you guys in?"

Emily exchanged glances with Jagger. She didn't know for sure how to answer that one. Thankfully, he caught the hint and answered smoothly, "As big a hurry as money can buy. I've been recalled to my unit and they'll reimburse me whatever it costs."

Don perked up. "You military? What service are you in?"

"Marines. I'm stationed at Quantico."

Emily stared. Seriously? How come he'd never mentioned that during their magical night together?

Don nodded. "Thought so. You have the look about you."

Jagger leaned an elbow on the counter as if to settle in for a chat. "You ex-military?"

Don replied eagerly, "I'm ex-army. Pulled a couple tours flying choppers with the Rangers in Iraq before I got shot. Bum knee now. Had to get out."

Jagger winced in sympathy. "Too bad. What're you flying now?"

"Sweet little Lear jet. I shuttle the AbaCo folks in and out mostly. Couple a' rich guys on the other side of Lokaina use me to fly to Tokyo once a month. They have a standing date with some geishas."

"Cool. Have you got extended-range fuel tanks on it to make the Japan run?"

"Yup. Just upgraded the avionics, too…"

Emily tuned out as the men talked airplanes and electronics. She recognized the male bonding ritual for what it was and let it take its course, even though her skin was crawling with dread and her gut screamed at her for them to get moving. *Now.*

Before she knew it, Don had offered to take Jagger out to the ramp to have a look at his jet. She tagged along without comment. She saw now where Jagger was taking this. Clever.

Sure enough, they spent about five minutes crawling all over the sleek plane, and Don piped up, "Hey, if we top off the tanks, I could fly you to the big island tonight. I haven't been drinking and I'm not sleepy. I'd have to charge you for a hotel room at that end, but I'm up for it. Whaddaya say?"

Jagger grinned. "Awesome. Any chance I can sit in the copilot seat for the takeoff if I promise not to touch anything?"

"Absolutely."

Emily rolled her eyes as the two men fueled the plane together and talked vintage sports cars. Gearheads, both of them. Strangely enough, she thought she registered a note of strain creeping into Jagger's voice. And he seemed to be favoring his right side a little. As though maybe he'd hurt it when the boat had exploded around him and the pain was just now starting to set in. Which made sense.

Almost dying must have sent his adrenaline sky-high. It would've taken a while to wear off.

Don took about a half hour to finish refueling, file a flight plan and preflight the plane. And then they were rolling down the runway and leaping into the air as the jet engines surged behind her. It was strange being all alone in the back of the plane. She was used to being crammed in a corner with a bunch of burly AbaCo employees jammed in around her.

When the plane reached cruising altitude, Jagger crawled out of the cockpit and came back to check on her. At least that was what he said. But she noticed a line of white around his mouth and the slight hitch that had entered his breathing.

"Are you hurt?" she murmured.

"A little."

"How little?" she retorted sharply. "Lemme see. It's your side, isn't it? I noticed you pressing your elbow against it earlier." She reached for his shirt.

He protested, pushing her hands away, but she persisted. "Don't you mess with me, Super

Spy. Pull your shirt up and let me have a look before I tackle you and make you do it," she threatened.

That brought a grin to his face. "You and what army, Danger Girl?"

"If AbaCo can't keep a hold of you, I doubt anyone can," she retorted.

Dang. She should've thought before she blurted that out. Her comment wiped the smile from his face and put back the heavy frown that had been momentarily missing. For a few minutes there, he'd almost looked like her old Jagger again.

Reluctantly, he lifted his shirt.

She gasped. A long, jagged piece of what looked like fiberglass was impaled in his right side. The piece came out of his back about two inches below his ribs. "Oh, my God," she cried in horror.

He looked down and grimaced. "I don't think it's as bad as it looks. I'm still breathing reasonably well."

Twin trails of blood trickled down his front and back from the two exit wounds.

"You're bleeding," she declared. "You've got to get to a hospital right away!"

Her exclamation drew Don's attention from the cockpit. He swore and unbuckled his seat belt. He joined them in the back, eyeing the injury.

Emily asked, "Uh, Don, if you're back here, who's flying the plane?"

"The autopilot." Then he turned to Jagger and said briskly, "Take off your shirt and lie down in the aisle here on your side so I can get a better look at that."

Jagger did as ordered. "You a medic?" he gritted out from between teeth that were definitely clenched now.

"Naw, but all us Rangers got decent combat first-aid training." The pilot leaned down to take a closer look at the white fragment.

It was nearly a foot long and roughly two inches wide.

Don asked lightly, "You get jumped by a canoe in a bar fight, dude?"

Jagger's pale lips turned up. "Yeah. It was a

hell of fight, but you ought to see the boat. I tore it to shreds."

Don announced, "We can't move the shrapnel. Don't want you to bleed out accidentally. You're gonna want a doctor to do that in case you punctured something major. I can't believe your lung hasn't collapsed. That thing goes right across the top of your diaphragm."

She winced. She could seriously do without the medically accurate blow-by-blow.

Don moved to a narrow closet behind the cockpit and rummaged around in it. He emerged with a first-aid kit. "This ain't much, but I can at least sterilize the wounds and pack 'em. Stop the worst blood loss for now. Nearest hospital's on Ranauatu Atoll. It's about an hour's flight from here. It's more of a clinic than a hospital, but they're 'bout all that's nearby for medical care."

Jagger hissed as the pilot blotted peroxide directly onto the wounds. Then he gritted out, "No hospital for me. Sorry."

She stared at him, appalled. "Why not?" It

was more an exclamation of disbelief than an actual question.

Jagger answered her nonetheless. "I don't trust AbaCo. They'll have people on the payrolls of any hospital, government offices—" His glance flickered to Don. "They probably pay Don here to keep them apprised of strangers coming and going from the area."

The pilot grinned, unabashed. "They pay stupid big amounts of money for me to do it, too. But funny, I have a hell of a hard time remembering to mention when marines pass through."

"Thanks, man," Jagger ground out.

Don sat down in an empty seat, staring down at Jagger on the floor thoughtfully. "Speaking of marines…there's a guy…'bout halfway back to the main islands…ex-marine. Owns a little island with a dirt strip on it. I think someone told me once that he was a field medic in Vietnam. He could probably handle an itty-bitty piece of shrapnel like that. Want me to radio him?"

Itty-bitty, her butt. That thing was the length of her forearm!

Jagger started to shrug, then broke off, sucking in a sharp breath. "It's worth a try."

In short order, Don had radioed the guy, explained the situation and altered their course. In about forty more minutes, he began a descent and quietly told Emily to buckle up. Jagger stayed on the floor, lying on his side. He'd gone quiet and had sucked down every painkiller in the first aid kit. Worse, he'd gone pale under the small overhead lights and his breathing had taken on a raspy quality.

The medic, a silver-haired man who introduced himself only as Lyle, met them at the plane with a golf cart. He and Don helped Jagger lie down across its backseat while Emily climbed in the front.

Don commented, "There's no air traffic coverage out here and nobody'll ever know about this little stop. So you two rest up, and when you're ready to go, you gimme a holler."

Jagger nodded. He seemed to be struggling to maintain consciousness now.

Don moved to her side and murmured, "I'm gonna fly on to Hawaii and build a cover story for you two there, but I'll need your credit card. I'll charge the room to it." He added drolly, "And I promise not to max it out, Mom."

She grinned and dug in her wallet. "Do your worst with it, Don. Max it out if you want. It's not nearly thanks enough for your help."

The ex-chopper pilot ducked his head. "Pshaw. Ain't nothing for a fellow marine. You take good care of him, ma'am."

The medic murmured, "We need to get going. This young man's trying to get shocky on me."

Don nodded and stepped back as the golf cart lurched into motion. Jagger moaned from behind her.

Emily whispered, "Hurry, Lyle. I can't lose him. Not after I just found him again."

Chapter 8

How she and Lyle horsed a now unconscious Jagger up the steps and into the ex-marine's kitchen, she had no idea. Adrenaline-induced superstrength, probably. But they managed to lay him out on his uninjured side on the kitchen table, which was covered with a clean sheet and brightly lit by several floor lamps with the shades removed. A kettle bubbled merrily on the stove, presumably for sterilizing surgical instruments. She didn't want to know.

Lyle went to work immediately, giving Jagger an injection of something and then cutting away the field dressing Don had put over the twin wounds. He told her, "Grab his shoulder and hold him down if he starts to thrash around."

She did as ordered while Lyle probed the wounds. A gush of blood made her turn her head away, her stomach roiling. Jagger groaned once but made no other protest as Lyle worked quickly. He picked up a scalpel and commenced cutting into Jagger's side. She handed the medic various implements as he asked for them. A ferrous smell of blood permeated the air.

"Dunno how this didn't catch his lung. Damned lucky," Lyle muttered to himself. Then, "Dirty as hell. Sure to get infected. Gonna need more antibiotics."

He didn't sound as though he expected a response from her, so she offered none. Besides, her teeth were clenched too tightly together to speak. And then it was done. An enormous length of bloody fiberglass lay on the table beside Jagger, the bleeders were cauterized, the wounds were stitched and bandaged and Lyle mopped sweat off his forehead.

"Thirsty?" the older man asked her casually.

She turned away from the hellish remains of the surgery. "Is he gonna be okay?"

Lyle shrugged. "He looks tough."

"That's not an answer."

"Here's the thing, Miss Grainger. The shrapnel didn't clip any major organs or blood vessels. That's the good news. The bad news is the wounds were filthy. He's bound to pick up the mother of all infections. He's lost a lot of blood, and he looks malnourished. That's the worst news of all."

"Can't you load him up on antibiotics and… and protein drinks or something?"

Lyle grinned. "In the morning I'll go to town and see if I can sweet-talk the doc there out of some Zithromax. May have to claim I've picked up the clap to get it." He grinned over at her. "I hate to wreck my sterling reputation like that, but for a fellow marine…"

Man, these marines took the whole brotherhood thing seriously! She nodded gratefully. "Is there anything we can do for him tonight?"

Lyle shrugged. "Let him sleep off the morphine I shot him up with. You look like you could use a shower and some shut-eye yourself."

Now that he mentioned it, exhaustion dragged at her eyelids until she could hardly hold them open. She kept the shower short and cool lest she fall asleep in it. As soon as she'd pulled on the clean, oversized T-shirt Lyle had laid out for her, she stumbled into the living room in search of sleep.

She noticed vaguely that the rustic cabin looked native Hawaiian. The ceilings were high-beamed and looked covered with some sort of dried leaves that formed a thatch over-head. There was no glass in the windows, just wooden shutters that closed over the spaces. Indeed, a pleasant trade wind blew through now. Just cool enough to need the light blanket Lyle handed her with a pillow. She'd insisted on curling up in the armchair beside the couch they'd moved Jagger to.

She slept deeply, dreaming of smiling blue eyes and fires burning on water.

In what seemed like only minutes, she awoke

to something kicking her foot. Sharply. She blinked her eyes open and stared, horrified.

Lyle was pointing a gun at her. He didn't look amused.

Ohmigod. She and an unconscious Jagger were alone on a rock with a madman! Or worse, had Don delivered them right into the clutches of Jagger's captors? Again? Sick terror washed through her.

"Uh, what's up, Lyle?" she mumbled.

"Care to tell me why the FBI's put out an APB on our patient?"

What? The FBI? But…but Jagger worked for the federal government. Why would they want to arrest their own man? Had he been lying to her about who he was? Had AbaCo been in the right to hold him prisoner?

Questions piled on top of questions in her fuzzy brain. Whom to trust? Whom to believe? Follow her head or her heart?

She asked carefully, "If you don't mind my asking, what are the charges against Jagger?"

Lyle shrugged. "The APB says he's a violent criminal. Attacked and killed a couple guys from some shipping company and is wanted in connection with smuggling and selling government secrets."

Okay, one thing she knew about Jagger Holtz. He would never sell out anyone he worked for. He was nothing if not loyal. Suddenly certainty flowed through her. "The charges are fake."

Lyle snorted. "Girlie, I hooked directly into the FBI Web site. There's nothing fake about the charges against the man lying on my couch."

She shook her head. "The people who tried to kill Jagger, they must've planted incriminating information against him when he escaped from them. They can't afford to have him tell the U.S. government what he knows about them, so they've trumped up these charges against him to force him not to testify against them."

"And is that how you explain the warrant for your arrest, too?"

"*My* arrest?"

Lyle nodded. "The complaint against you says you broke into this shipping company's records. Says you broke into sealed cargo containers, too, and violated international customs laws."

She sighed. "Well, those charges are true. But I did it to free Jagger. He was locked up in a cargo container on a ship for two years. I found him and let him out." As Lyle stared in shock, she added defiantly, "I'd do it again, too. Even if it means I have to go to jail."

The marine studied her closely and eventually nodded. "You're telling the truth. Maybe you two have been set up." He glanced over at Jagger's bandaged form. "And I've got to admit that boy's injuries look like the kind you get when someone is trying to kill you, not when you're trying to kill someone else."

She commenced breathing again as Lyle lowered the weapon and eased the hammer of his pistol back into place. He said firmly, "You go on back to sleep."

As if that was going to happen anytime soon! Her heart was still stuck somewhere in the vicinity of her throat.

He continued, "I'm heading to town to get more medical supplies. I'll be back in a few hours. Keep your boy still and give him water if he wakes up and asks for it."

She listened until a motorboat retreated in the distance. Was Lyle heading to the nearest town with police in it to report them? Would he return with a squad of AbaCo men? She sighed. It wasn't as though she could do a darned thing about it now. Jagger was still unconscious on the couch. And even if he could move, where would they go? They were on an island in the middle of nowhere.

What were the two of them going to do? The U.S. government believed Jagger was a traitor, and she'd become a wanted criminal. Who would help them now? If only he'd wake up. Maybe he'd know how to proceed. But what if he didn't? What if there was no way out of this mess?

She must have fretted herself to sleep eventually because a moan ripped her from a troubled dream some time later. She jolted upright. Jagger was thrashing on the couch, swearing up a blue storm.

She leaped to his side. "Hey, cool it or else you'll rip out your stitches."

Unfocused eyes stared up at her. "I'll never talk. You understand? Never. I know you're going to do whatever you have to, and I'm going to scream and suffer and you're going to do even more to me. But at the end of the day, you're getting nothing from me. Just so we're clear on that."

He must be dreaming about his captivity.

And then she knew it because he started to scream. It wasn't a high-pitched sound of fright like a woman reacting to a mouse. This scream came from the depths of his gut, torn from his throat, raw and feral in its agony. Right then and there, her knees collapsed out from under her. She needed no further explanation of what had happened to him as AbaCo's prisoner. That one scream said it all.

She leaned forward, grabbing Jagger's shoulders as he twisted back and forth, begging him to stay still. She practically had to sit on him to slow him down, and he cursed at her all the while. And the things he ranted about in his delirium…the torture he described…the days on end alone and isolated…his longing for decent food or for just a glimpse of sunlight…

Bit by bit, he tore her heart out as she pieced together the story of his past two years in his ramblings. It was hard for her to believe that AbaCo could do that to anyone and get away with it. But it was even harder to believe he'd survived it all. His mental and physical toughness, his raw courage, his sheer, ferocious will to live boggled her mind.

She heard a motorboat returning and her pulse leaped. She clutched Jagger's hand tightly, still registering how hot and dry it was in her panic.

The kitchen door opened.

Nobody shouted for her to put her hands over her head. No gang of armed men rushed into the room.

Lyle's craggy visage poked around the door. "Any change in your fellow while I was gone?"

She all but sobbed in relief. "He thrashed around for a while and he's been talking in his sleep."

"Fever's setting in. He's going delirious on us. Lemme go get my bag of goodies."

Emily hovered, feeling in turns helpless and protective as Lyle started an IV drip on Jagger, rigging the saline bag to one of the floor lamps from the kitchen last night. Into it, the medic injected a cocktail of antibiotics and sedatives. And then he ordered her to take another shower, announcing that she still stunk like rotten seaweed.

Under other circumstances, she'd have savored the hot rainwater, sluicing the remaining salt off her skin and out of her hair. But today she raced through her shower, impatient to get back to Jagger.

He was quiet through the day and into the night. But late in the evening, his temperature started to rise once more.

"Here it comes," Lyle announced grimly. "The primary infection. We're in for a fight, girl, if we want to save your man."

She sat up with Jagger through the night, her panic rising exponentially along with his fever. Funny how just a few days ago she was so mad at him she could hardly stand to think about him. And now here she was, praying nonstop for him to pull through this crisis.

Just when she thought she had life all figured out, it went and threw a monster curveball at her. She spent hours staring at Jagger's face, rememorizing the planes and angles, sharper now, but still the old Jagger. The new lines and shadows gave him more character, an added maturity that was intensely appealing.

Lyle had told her to expect Jagger to say all sorts of crazy things and not to freak out over it. Thing was, Lyle had no idea that most of what Jagger talked about *was* real. That was a burden she got to bear alone.

Lyle took his turns looking after Jagger so she could catch a nap now and then, and he ordered her to wake him up if Jagger's temperature hit one hundred and five.

When it was just her and Jagger alone in the quietest, darkest heart of the night, her thoughts strayed to the first time she'd spent a night with him, that magical New Year's Eve two years ago. It had been about as different from this as was possible. But the sense of rightness, of peace way down deep in her soul at just being with him, remained the same. She didn't know what it was about him, but she'd never met another man like him. He was simply meant for her and she for him. There was no logic to it, no reason for it. It just was.

She'd spent the past two years fighting this thing between them, but after a single day back in his company, the old attraction was back full force. And this time they had so much more between them. Not that he was aware of it at the moment, of course. After he beat this infection she would tell him all about it. And maybe they could properly celebrate the past two New Year's Eves they'd missed.

Of course, first he had to live. His temperature climbed steadily to one hundred and four degrees and then passed up the mark. And that was when he began to talk again. At first it was just mumbled words and phrases. And then his rantings began to take shape. He muttered her name several times.

She leaned over him and whispered, "I'm here, Jagger."

"Bitch," he muttered.

She stared, shocked.

"Set me up…great actress…actually believed she gave a damn about me…alone so long in my job and then she came along…so inno-cent…but it was a lie…led me right to you bas-tards…"

She recoiled in horror. *No. It can't be. It's just the fever talking.*

"If I ever find her…"

"What, Jagger? What will you do if you find her?"

"Kill her…no…too easy. Make her suffer… Yeah, suffer…"

Oh. My. God. He couldn't possibly believe she'd set him up on that New Year's Eve two years ago! But as he continued to mutter about how she'd been in league with his kidnappers and had served him up to them on a silver plat-ter, it was clear that was exactly what he did believe.

She spoke urgently. "Listen to me, Jagger. I

didn't set you up. I swear. I had no part of Aba-Co's goons kidnapping you. We met by chance and I was crazy about you."

His head turned back and forth restlessly. "No chance about it," he mumbled. "I needed into that party…I approached the girl… thought she'd be such an easy mark…I never dreamed…"

Emily sat back, frowning. Was *she* the girl he was referring to? Memory of him standing in that parking garage waiting for the elevator flashed through her head. He'd been using her? She tried again to penetrate his delirium, asking forcefully, "Jagger, what were you going to use me for?"

"Had to find our men. AbaCo snatched them…need proof to move on the company… grand jury wants some evidence before they get involved…"

AbaCo had kidnapped someone else? Were these other men riding around the world in cargo containers, lost and forgotten, too? "Who were they?" she asked.

Jagger sat bolt upright and his eyes popped

open. The expression in them was wild. Unfocused. "Gotta find them!" he burst out.

"Lie back down, Jagger," she soothed. "We'll find your colleagues when you're feeling better. I promise." She'd learned the hard way over the past several hours that she wasn't anywhere near strong enough to force Jagger to do anything. With a little more cajoling from her, he finally lay back down.

She smoothed his damp hair off his brow, worried by the fine sheen of perspiration there. She stuck the electronic thermometer in his ear again. Up another tenth of a degree, 104.5. She pondered waking Lyle, but the medic had gotten practically no sleep last night and wasn't exactly a spring chicken. He'd mentioned trying to bathe Jagger to help cool him, but it was imperative that his wounds stay dry.

Inspiration struck. She headed for the kitchen and rummaged around until she found a mixing bowl. She filled it with water and ice and then snagged every dish towel she could find.

She soaked a towel in cold water and laid it

across Jagger's chest. She folded another wet towel and laid it across his forehead. Another one across his hips below the bandages, several more on his legs. By the time she laid the last one across his feet, the first one on his chest was warm to the touch. She dipped it in the cold water, wrung it out and replaced it.

Jagger's body was much as she remembered, powerful and lean, brimming with vitality, even in his current state. As she worked, though, she spotted a myriad of new scars. And something hot and demanding began to build in her belly. *Rage.*

A thin scar on his neck looked like some sort of slashing wound. His captors must have toyed with slitting his throat. Several small round scars clustered on his belly looked like cigarette burns. Then she found a whole series of tiny marks on his back over both kidneys. She recalled hearing somewhere that the most painful form of torture was to stick needles in the human kidney. Apparently, the nerves from the incredibly sensitive organ were wired to the brain so a human couldn't pass out from that pain. And then she found the scars on the bottoms of his feet. Dozens of them. Scars on top of scars. The width of her finger in a criss-crossing pattern as though they'd caned his feet bloody. More than once. Many times more than once.

And that was when her rage spilled over.

She was going to kill someone for this. No, Jagger had the right of it. She was going to hurt someone very badly and *then* kill them. How could anyone visit this sort of damage on another human being? Whoever'd done this to Jagger didn't deserve to live. She'd track them down. Hunt them herself if she had to.

No wonder Jagger was so furious with her if he thought she'd had some part in doing this to him. Frankly, she was amazed that he was only enraged. How had he clung to sanity at all? New awe at his mental and physical endurance filled her.

She continued draping him in cool towels all through the night. His temperature stabilized at 104.5, but he continued to drift in and out, sometimes still and apparently asleep, and other times mumbling and tossing. And some-time during that endless night, the worst of her rage settled into grim resolve to help Jagger find his captors and do whatever he wanted to them. But first he had to live.

A little before dawn, Lyle came into the living room to check on his patient.

"How's he doing?" Emily asked anxiously.

Lyle shrugged noncommittally. "The next twenty-four hours will tell the tale. Go get some sleep and I'll take over towel duty. Good idea, by the way."

As skeptical as she was that she'd get any sleep, she lay down in Lyle's bed—the only bed in the house—and closed her eyes. She awoke to brilliant sunlight streaming through the window into her face. Shading her eyes, she glanced over at the alarm clock and was stunned to see it read nearly noon. She jumped up and rushed out to see how Jagger was doing.

She frowned. His head was lying in the mixing bowl she'd used earlier, and the thing was half-filled with ice water. "Are you wash-ing his hair?" she asked in surprise.

Lyle glanced up grimly. "No. I'm trying to keep his brain from frying. His temperature spiked about an hour ago, and we've got to keep his head cool or he'll get brain damage. Go get me another tray of ice, will you?"

She headed for the kitchen. Dismayed, she stared at the array of shallow bowls and plates of half-frozen water now filling the freezer along with several ice-cube trays. Lyle must think this fever wasn't going away anytime soon. She grabbed a tray of ice cubes and rushed back to Jagger's side.

She worked towel duty while Lyle dumped the ice cubes in Jagger's head bath. "How long do you think this fever will last?" she asked.

"Until it breaks or he dies."

Dread filled her, as icy as the water bathing Jagger. "When will we know which way this is gonna go?"

Lyle frowned. "I've seen a lot of wounds go septic. Guys usually last a day. Maybe two at most."

"Isn't there anything you can do?" she cried.

"I doubled up the antibiotics this morning. I'm giving him all the help I can."

"I'll call Don to come get him. Fly him out to the nearest hospital." Frantically, she fumbled for her cell phone before she remembered it had been ruined in the ocean.

Lyle shook his head. "Boy's too sick to move. The flight would kill him. Besides, there's not much more a hospital could do for him. They have fancy refrigerated blankets to help hold down fevers, but your towels will work nearly as well. They'd give him the same medications I am, and then they'd wait just like we are. If you want to do something more to help, say a prayer."

Lyle enlisted her to help to change the dressing on Jagger's wounds, and she flinched to see the angry red swelling around them. The medic commented, "I'd open those up and clean 'em again, but the kid can't afford to lose any more blood than he already has." He shook his head direly.

Emily piped up, "My blood is O positive. Anyone can take that type, can't they?"

"Yeah," Lyle answered cautiously.

"You've got needles and tubes and all that intravenous stuff, right? Take a pint of my blood and give it to Jagger. That way you can clean out his wounds."

Lyle studied her speculatively. "Any chance you've got AIDS or hepatitis?"

She shook her head in the negative. "Haven't had an injection or slept with a guy in two years and I don't do drugs."

"It might be worth a try. He's not doing so great."

"Do it," she urged. "Please. We've got to do everything we can."

"All right. Lemme go sterilize up some needles."

In a few minutes, Lyle came back with a big glass of orange juice in hand. "Drink this. I don't need you passing out on me, too. One sick patient at a time is enough for me."

She downed the juice quickly.

Lyle explained, "I'm gonna stick you and then plug you directly into his IV."

She winced at the needle stick in the bend

of her elbow, but in a matter of seconds, the clear tube turned dark red as her blood began streaming into Jagger's arm. Satisfaction filled her. This felt right. Her life force flowing into him, becoming part of him. Lyle timed the transfer carefully.

"There. That's about a pint," he announced.

She actually felt bereft when he disconnected her from Jagger. But then Lyle drafted her to assist while he carefully snipped the stitches and lanced the wounds. She did her best to block out seeing what emerged from the wounds. Suffice it to say it was a good thing that Lyle opened Jagger back up again. The amount of blood was alarming, but eventually it ran a healthy red, and Lyle stitched Jagger up once more.

Maybe it was the blood she'd donated, but she felt utterly drained both physically and emotionally by the time it was over. Jagger was more pale than ever and utterly still now. She almost wished for the return of the thrashing and ranting. At least then she knew he was still alive, still fighting. But this deeply unconscious state of his was the most frightening of all.

He was the same through the evening, lying zombielike on the sofa without so much as a twitch. Lyle's expression went from grim to grave. She was losing him. Jagger was slipping away before her very eyes. She prayed and then she cried and then she prayed some more. She felt so damned helpless! Surely there was something she could do.

Around midnight, his breathing started to labor, coming in painful rasps. She called out, "Lyle, do something!"

The medic came in from the kitchen and examined Jagger yet again. Then the man said gently, "Honey, there's nothing more we can do. It's up to God and Jagger now. Either he has something to live for, some work left undone here on earth, or it's his time to go."

And that was when she knew exactly what she had to do. "Could I have a moment alone with him?"

The older man nodded and stepped outside onto the porch. The door closed behind him.

She knelt by Jagger's side and took one of his hot, limp hands in hers. She put her mouth close to his ear. "Do you need something to live for? Well, try this on for size. That night we spent together two years ago? New Year's Eve, remember? You and I have a daughter, Jagger. Her name is Michelle. She's fifteen months old and looks just like you. And she deserves to meet her daddy someday. Don't you die on her. You fight, by God. You *live*—you hear me? You owe it to her. You left us before, but now you've come back to us. Don't you dare leave us again."

Chapter 9

Jagger gradually became aware of floating within a peaceful silence. It cocooned him gently in a white, weightless mist. It was a nice change from the constant dark and he was in no rush to get back to the real world. But eventually, he couldn't resist checking in on reality and opened his eyes.

He squinted into bright sunlight. That was odd. He was awake, but he wasn't in his box. What were his captors up to now?

Someone moved nearby. He looked off to his left and saw a strange man approaching. He surged up, then collapsed back, gasping as hot knives of crumpling agony stabbed his left side.

"Easy, kid. I'm one of the good guys," the stranger soothed. "But I'm gonna be pissed if I have to stitch up your side again."

The man sounded American. All of his AbaCo captors had been distinctly German. Suspiciously, Jagger asked, "How do I know you're one of the good guys?"

The man frowned. "That's a good question. How 'bout this?" He shoved up his sleeve to reveal a Marine Corps eagle, globe and anchor tattoo on his left biceps. "Don't know too many bad guys sporting one of these."

Jagger sagged back to the cushions in relief. *"Semper fi,"* he sighed.

"Semper fidelis, my young friend. Lemme go wake up Emily. She's gonna be over the moon that you're coming around. Girl's been sitting up with you practically around the clock."

The gray-haired man left the room before Jagger could ask any more questions. Emily was here? He'd have pegged her for the type to cut and run when the shooting started. And she'd been sitting with him around the clock? Why? How long had he been out of it, anyway?

Two years ago, he'd have described the pain in his left side as excruciating. But now... now he'd classify it as annoying but tolerable. Funny how pain was all a matter of perspective.

"Jagger?" Emily rushed into the room, her hair sticking up every which way. It was actually incredibly cute. She looked like a rumpled kitten. "Are you really awake? How do you feel?" To the older man she blurted, "Has the fever truly broken?"

The marine grinned. "Yup, 102.1 and dropping."

Fever? He'd been sick, then? He felt as if he'd been run over a couple of times by a Mack truck.

She moved to his side, smiling down brilliantly at him—in relief if he wasn't mistaken. "I *knew* you'd make it."

She said that as though it had been in serious doubt. He asked, frowning, "How sick was I?"

The man answered, "'Bout as sick as I've ever seen anyone be and still live. That was a hell of an infection you got, boy. Had to lance your wounds twice. Finally had to install tubes in 'em to drain 'em."

Wounds? Plural? "What's wrong with me?" he asked in alarm.

The man said, "Name's Lyle, by the way. Marine medic, 'Nam, '66 to '72. You took a piece of fiberglass through your left side. I've got it in the kitchen if you want a souvenir. 'Bout the size of a bowie knife blade. Did about as much damage as one, too."

Jagger reached gingerly for his side and encountered heavy white gauze wrappings.

"Easy, son. Tubes are still in. Shrapnel missed your lung by a hair. Tore up your diaphragm—breathing may be a bit hard for a few weeks. Don't run any marathons for a couple months, okay?"

Jagger nodded. Now that the immediate concern for his health was past, the next pressing concern was… "Where in the hell am I?" he blurted.

Emily fielded this one. "When we realized you were hurt and you refused to go to a hospital, Don diverted his plane into this island so Lyle could look after you."

Jagger glanced over at Lyle, who added, "I own this chunk of rock. It's just a pretty little spot in the middle of nowhere."

From a box to a rock. Jagger supposed that was a step up.

Lyle continued. "Stay as long as you like. It's kinda nice having some company for a change."

Jagger nodded cautiously. Don. The name sounded familiar. But he wasn't putting a face with it. Last thing he remembered, he was driving a boat across the open ocean with no land in sight anywhere. Fuzzy recollection of an explosion throwing him high into the sky tickled at his memory, but that could be from a dozen war zones he'd fought in over the years.

Emily's palm was cool against his forehead. "He still feels warm," she said worriedly.

Lyle shrugged. "It may be another day or two before the fever's completely gone. We're still gonna have to watch for relapses for a few days."

Emily nodded and glanced down. "Are you hungry, Jagger?"

"Yeah. I guess I am."

Lyle cautioned, "Go easy on 'im. Start with something simple like chicken noodle soup. He'll need to work his way up to your world-famous enchiladas."

Emily grinned. "Aha. The truth comes out. You just want us to stay for my cooking."

"Damn straight, girl." Lyle laughed.

Jagger never dreamed that a simple bowl of soup could taste so good. Maybe it was the not eating for several days. Maybe it was two years of tough jerky and rotting fruit and tasteless oatmeal. But either way, he savored each and every drop of the rich broth. And then came orange juice. Surely it was God's own nectar. He'd never tasted anything so zesty and re-freshing.

Lyle helped him to his feet a little while later and guided him to the restroom. Afterward, he noticed a door that looked as if it led outside. Jagger murmured, "Any chance I can step out for a minute? It's been a long time since I saw the sun."

Lyle threw him a knowing look. "I was one of the medics who repatriated POWs in Germany when they came out of 'Nam. If you wanna talk, I've heard it all."

Jagger nodded. He wasn't ready for an amateur shrink quite yet. He just wanted to feel sunlight on his skin before this dream faded away and was replaced by the harsh, cold reality of another crate.

An ocean breeze caressed his skin as he stepped onto a long, covered porch. Emily was already out there sprawling in a chair, eyes closed and face lifted to the sun.

"Hey," he murmured as he eased gently into the chair beside her.

Her eyes flew open. "Should you be up and about yet?"

He shrugged. "Lyle didn't stop me from coming out here."

They sat together in silence for a time. It was tranquil. The sound of the waves a hundred yards away was soothing. He'd gotten so sick of listening to water over the past two years, he was surprised to find it pleasant today.

"How much do you remember of the past few days?" she eventually asked cautiously.

"Not much. Why?"

"Just wondering."

He frowned, suspicions aroused. That was the sort of question people asked when they were hinting around about something. There was more to it than idle curiosity. What was she worried about him remembering?

She distracted him by murmuring, "You talked a fair bit in your delirium."

Delirium? Holy— "Did I say anything interesting?"

"You said quite a few interesting things. You talked about your captivity mostly." She hesitated and then added, "When I was draping you in cold towels, I saw your scars."

Ah. Mentally, he winced. He'd figured at the time he picked up most of the injuries that he'd be pretty much done with the ladies after his ordeal was over. No woman would find his freakishly scarred body attractive. His captors had marred him pretty much from head to toe.

"It's an impressive collection," she commented neutrally.

"Impressive? Is that what you'd call it?" he asked bitterly.

In a flash she was on her knees before him. He stared down at her, startled.

"Jagger, I *swear* I had absolutely nothing to do with your capture. I had no knowledge of it and I didn't set you up. I was furious, in fact. I thought you ditched me the morning after— well, you know what after."

He stared down at her skeptically. Words were cheap. Just because she said so didn't mean he ought to believe her. But there was something…hovering just beyond recollection. Something important that happened during his fever. Did it have something to do with this? The gaping hole in his memory was frustrating.

"Does Lyle have a telephone?" he asked.

She shook her head. "But he has an Internet hookup if you want to e-mail someone. Friends or family…" She broke off leadingly as if she was fishing for information about his personal life.

"I was thinking about my superiors, actually. They must think I'm dead by now."

"Uh, there may be a problem with that."

Here it came. The smooth redirect to keep him from contacting any outsiders to let someone know he wasn't shark bait.

"It seems that AbaCo planted some false information with the FBI about you and me. Well, false in your case. The stuff on me is true. But anyway, there are federal warrants out for both our arrests."

As annoying as that was, he couldn't say he was entirely surprised. It was definitely AbaCo's style. "I still need to contact my superiors. The only way we're going to straighten this out is to talk to them."

"Jagger, I can't stand by and watch you go from one jail cell to another!" She sounded genuinely distraught at the prospect. He had to admit, he wasn't crazy about the idea, either.

But at least in an American jail he'd have decent food and some rights.

"Where's the computer?" he asked determinedly.

When he made to stand up, Emily was there instantly, supporting his right elbow. Damn, he was weak. With her help, he managed to totter into the house. He sat down at the computer in the corner of the kitchen and typed out a short message from Lyle's e-mail account to his headquarters in Quantico reporting that he was alive and would return to make a full report and clear his name as soon as he was strong enough to do so. There was no immediate response. He realized belatedly that if it was late afternoon here in the Pacific, it must be the middle of the night in Virginia.

He headed for the couch, inexplicably exhausted. Or maybe not so inexplicably. He caught a glance of a substantial shard of fiberglass on the kitchen counter. It did, indeed, remind him of a cross between a wicked knife and a small machete. And that thing had punctured him through? No wonder he'd almost croaked.

He lay down, grateful to rest, and it was morning the next time he awoke, with the sun streaming in from the other side of the room. Emily dozed in a chair beside him but roused the moment he shifted his weight.

She poked a thermometer in his ear. "Ninety-nine point nine," she announced. "You're almost back to human again."

"Is that why I'm so hungry I could eat the arm of this sofa?"

She grinned. "What's your pleasure? Pancakes? Eggs and bacon?"

"Do you know how to make French toast?" he asked.

"Coming right up."

In short order, she carried in a big plate of French toast, swimming in butter and confectioners' sugar and dribbled with syrup. She'd already cut it into neat little bite-sized pieces for him. Cripes. She was treating him like a four-year-old. But when he shifted to sit up, he froze as searing pain impaled him.

Emily winced along with him. "Lyle discontinued the morphine drip last night. He was worried about you getting hooked on it. He said you'd be a little sore this morning."

Jagger snorted.

She grinned commiseratingly. "Actually, I believe his exact words were that you'd hurt like a son of a bitch today."

"He wasn't wrong," Jagger managed to grit out.

He didn't complain when she lifted a forkful of French toast to his mouth for him. But he did groan—in pleasure—when he tasted it.

"It's the vanilla," she murmured. "Makes all the difference."

He didn't care if the secret ingredient was arsenic. This stuff was to die for. He ate every bite and then slept again.

For the next three days, he followed that pattern pretty much around the clock. Sleep. Eat. Soak up a little sun. Sleep again. And somewhere in there, he began to feel human. He was starting to gain a little weight if his face in the bathroom mirror was any indication. He didn't look quite so gaunt anymore. Emily delighted in cooking for him and spent hours in the kitchen whipping up some new delicacy each day.

He was actually starting to believe that maybe, just maybe, this wasn't some elaborate scheme by AbaCo to screw with his head.

And then Lyle hollered from the kitchen on the fourth morning, "You've got an e-mail, boy. You better come take a look at it."

He pushed up off the couch and went to the kitchen to read it over Lyle's shoulder. Emily was already there, frowning at the message.

Step outside at 10:16 a.m. Turn your face up to the sky.

"What's that about?" Lyle inquired.

"Satellite must be flying overhead then. They want to get a visual on me to see if it's really me."

"Jeez. You're telling me they can ID you from space?" the older man asked.

Jagger nodded. "Yup."

"The military's come a long way since my days in the service," Lyle grumbled.

Emily was grim. "How do we know this isn't from AbaCo? Maybe they're going to fly a helicopter over at that exact moment and shoot you."

"I thought I was supposed to be the paranoid one."

She scowled. "I lost you once before. I'm not losing you again."

Something clicked in his head. Those words. He'd heard her say something like that before. Sometime during that black hole in his memory. Bits and pieces of it were starting to come back. He remembered being chased by a black cigarette boat off the coast of Lokaina, now. He vaguely remembered the interior of a small business jet. And being unbearably thirsty.

He frowned, racking his brains for more to this new fragment of memory, but nothing came.

At 10:10 a.m. or so, he went outside. In bright daylight like this, he wasn't likely to spot the spy satellite crossing overhead. But he walked down to the dirt airstrip, which was the most open spot on the island, and looked up, certain the satellite was out there.

He stayed on the field until 10:30 a.m., and then he made his way back inside and sat down at the computer. He didn't have long to wait. The e-mail came through and he opened it immediately.

If you and your accomplice turn yourselves in immediately, the federal prosecutor will take that into account when he files his formal charges. A team is standing by at Quantico to conduct a full debrief and take your statement.

He groaned under his breath. He knew precisely what was entailed in a full debrief. Days of grueling interrogation, full-bore efforts to break down his story, sleep deprivation, emotional duress, whatever it took. But after Aba-Co's efforts to extract information from him, he highly doubted Uncle Sam could throw anything at him that would freak him out. But Emily—

The thought of her undergoing the same sort of browbeating made something growl way down deep in his gut. She was too innocent, too sweet, too damned soft to be put through something like that. As the gut feeling about her bubbled up into conscious thought, he froze. Was he falling for her again? Was home-cooking and a cool hand smoothing his brow all it took to make a complete sucker out of him?

Or was he a sucker at all? Was it possible that she was for real? Sometimes when he glanced over at her quickly, he caught pain in her big brown eyes. Pain for him. She bent over backward to make him comfortable, to anticipate his every need, to do little things constantly to show how much she cared for him. All of that went way above and beyond the call of acting concerned for him. It was hard to draw any other conclusion than the obvious one. She really did give a damn for him.

He turned his gaze back to that order, thinly

veiled, for him to get his butt back to Quantico and face the charges against him. He'd bet they were interested in hearing from him, all right.

He typed back, Will return as soon as able to give complete statement and answer all questions. Am recuperating from serious injuries sustained in my escape from captors. There. Let them chew on that.

"Everything okay?" Emily murmured.

"Just ducky," he replied, grinning.

She inhaled sharply and he looked up at her quickly. Her eyes were wide, and she was staring at him like a starstruck kid meeting a movie star. He raised an inquiring eyebrow.

She answered, "That's the first time you've really looked like the old Jagger. The one I met and fell—" she broke off "—the one I met two years ago."

She met and fell for? Was that how she was going to finish that sentence? Huh. It didn't matter. He shouldn't care. He *didn't* care. That was not pleasure spreading like warm honey in his gut.

He slept through most of the afternoon, but as the sun began to set, he woke, restless. "Walk with me, Emily," he murmured.

They headed down to the beach, where Mother Nature treated them to a spectacular sunset in shades of pink, peach, crimson, lavender and violet. He sat down in the warm sand as the last vestiges of the show faded from the sky.

Emily plopped down beside him.

Perhaps it was the prospect of returning to Virginia, or maybe he was just healing enough to face it now, but tonight his thoughts turned to his captivity and the grueling torture he'd endured.

He spoke quietly, without looking at her. "My captors told me you'd betrayed me. That you'd helped them set me up and had led me to them. They showed me pictures they had of the two of us at the party and surveillance pictures of us going into the hotel."

She gasped.

"I didn't believe them at first. I'd looked into your eyes. Held you in my arms. Hell, made love to you. There was no way you faked what I felt between us. But over time…" He took a steadying breath and continued. "You've got to understand. Being under that kind of physical and emotional pressure messes with your head. You start to believe stuff. Even crazy stuff. I believed them."

She made a sound of protest, but he waved her to silence. He wanted to get this off his chest.

"Funny thing is, I think maybe that's the one thing that kept me alive. I was so damned mad at you for playing me like that. There were times when my rage, my determination to find you and get even with you was the only thing that sustained me."

He stared out at the black ocean for a moment, searching for words. "So it's a little weird for me now, after hating you so passionately for two years, to suddenly find out that the one thing I was living for was all a lie."

She opened her mouth to say something, thought better of it and closed her mouth.

"What?" he asked. "Talk to me."

She smiled a sad little smile. "I feel a little stupid and a lot guilty about how mad I was at you for sneaking out the morning after like that. I swore never to speak to you again. To cut you completely out of my life, out of my thoughts—" her voice hitched "—out of my heart. I vowed to myself never to need you again. Never to ask anything of you."

When she didn't go on, he prompted, "And now?"

"And now it's all I can do not to fling myself at you and beg you never to leave me again. But I have no right. I did, in fact, work for the very people who did this to you. For all I know, they did use me without my knowledge to set you up. You'll never look at me and see anything other than a collaborator with your enemies."

He peered at her in the dusk, trying to make out the expression in her eyes. But she'd averted her face until all he saw was a glistening track down her cheek.

After a moment, she continued, "If there's anything I can do to help you catch the people who kidnapped you, I'll do it. No questions asked. Anything at all. Just say the word."

He turned over her words for a while. Finally he said gravely, "I do have one request of you."

"Name it."

"Kiss me."

Chapter 10

Emily inhaled sharply, stunned. "Seriously?"

He made a sound that was half laugh and half something else that sounded like pain. "For better or worse, I've been thinking about you nonstop for two years. Is it any surprise that the first woman I want to kiss now is you?"

Memory of his bitter words against her during his delirium flashed into her head. Was this some ploy to get inside her guard so he could take his long-sought revenge? Or was it the innocent request he made it sound like? Was she the paranoid one now—and did it matter?

Truth was, she'd desperately wanted to kiss him almost from the first moment she'd seen him again. Even if he was setting her up for a one-night stand with the intent to leave her high and dry for real this time, she didn't think she had it in her to say no to him. Her addiction to him ran too deep, too permanent, to deny. No matter what his motives were, she wasn't going to say no to kissing him once more.

She surrendered to her heart. "I guess it's not a surprise that you want to kiss me. I want to kiss you, too."

He smiled, but it was too dark to see if the smile reached his eyes or not. She rose to her knees and moved closer to him. And then very carefully, very slowly, she leaned forward. Their breath mingled and she paused, startled by intense recognition of the spicy scent. A cold night, a candlelit suite, an evening of magical seduction were all tied to that masculine aroma. The taste of it was potent and familiar on her tongue, more complex and delicious than any fine wine. Just like the man.

His fingertips touched her cheeks. Slid down her jaw to rest on her throat. Her whole body pulsed with awareness of him, undulating toward him, drawn like a magnet.

She tilted her head. Their lips touched.

Oh, my. His mouth was as warm and resilient and restless as she remembered. But there was more to him this time. A depth of experience. Wisdom and a measure of sadness hard-earned. Less of the devil-may-care recklessness. He was more of a man and less of a playboy. And absolutely irresistible because of it. She arched into him, her arms looping around his neck as need exploded inside her.

How could she ever have convinced herself she could cut this man out of her life? He was as much a part of her as her arms or her legs. More so. He was part of her soul.

His arms swept around her and he pushed her down gently to the sand, following her eagerly, their mouths never parting. Her lips opened and his tongue was there, tasting and testing, caressing and cajoling. Not that she needed any encouragement. His desperate urgency was contagious

"Are you real," he murmured against her lips, "or is this a dream?"

She ducked her head into his shoulder and laughed under her breath. "And here I was, asking myself the exact same thing. Does it matter?"

"Nope. I'll take it either way. This is a hell of a lot better than anything else I've dreamed in the past two years. Although there was that recurring dream about eating steak in a bubble bath…"

She replied playfully, "That can be arranged."

"Have you seen Lyle's bathtub? It looks like half a whiskey barrel. To sit in that thing I'd have to stick my knees up my nose. There's hardly room for bubbles, let alone you and a steak."

"Oh-ho! So the dream involved a girl in the tub, too, did it?"

Jagger grinned. "Well, yeah. You starred in many more of my dreams than I wanted."

She winced at the reminder that for the past two years he'd thought the absolute worst of her. "And now?"

"Oh, you're still in my dreams."

She whispered, "So let's make one of them real, shall we?"

His eyes went even darker and more turbulent than they already were. He lowered his mouth to hers and kissed her with restrained violence. And which dream of his was this? One where he seduced her with cold calculation and walked away with the pieces of her heart in his pocket, or one where they made sweet, tender love until they couldn't lift a finger between them? Sadly, she didn't care which. She'd take him any way she could get him.

His mouth and hands roamed over her body, burning her until the cool night air felt wonderful against her heated skin. Her cheeks must be cherry-red, they felt so hot. Her breasts, her belly, her entire body felt flushed and hypersensitive. She was abjectly grateful when he came up for air long enough to peel her out of her clothes and strip off his as well.

She murmured, "Did you ever imagine this with me in the past two years? A moonlit beach all to ourselves on a tropical island? Just the two of us, naked and together?"

His eyes closed in pain. "I didn't want to. I hated myself for thinking about it. But…yes." The hoarse word sounded torn from his gut. "Yes. I hated you for it, but I still wanted you."

"Me, too," she whispered. "I never stopped wanting you. I dreamed about you. About… doing things with you."

"Like what?" he asked against the tender flesh at the base of her ear.

His mouth made it nearly impossible for her to concentrate on an answer. She mumbled, "You know. Things."

"Tell me."

How could she refuse him? Not after all he'd been through. Not any more than she could deny a starving man food or a parched man water. "I imagined making love with you to the rhythm of waves crashing on a beach. Under the stars. Just the two of us. Free to do anything and everything we want to."

She felt his lips curve up in a smile against

the base of her throat. "Kind of like here and now?"

"Um, yes. Kind of exactly like this."

His fingers drifted down her side, along her thigh and curled around the back of her knee. "You know what they say. Sometimes dreams come true."

A low moan of need slipped out of her, and Jagger needed no further permission to proceed. He pulled her leg up over his hip, opening her to more intimate exploration. She tried to be careful of his bandages, but he was having no part of it.

At first, it was all skin and mouths and hands and frantic hurry. And then, as the reality of the moment set in for both of them—awareness…and then belief…that this wasn't a dream on the verge of slipping away at any second— they slowed down. Way down.

They lay side by side on the sand, gazing deep into each other's eyes, and ever so slowly reacquainted themselves with each other's bodies with languid hands and gentle mouths. She learned the new contours of his leaner form, while he explored the changes the past two years had wrought in her as well.

"You're curvier than I remembered," he murmured. "Less of a girl and more of a woman."

Alarm jabbed her. Not a place she wanted to go just yet. Not now. Not when the reason for her curviness had so much potential for strife. Instead, she laughed lightly. "Is that a polite way of telling me I've gotten fat?"

"Good Lord, no! It's a polite way of telling you that you've grown up. Become a beautiful woman in her prime. It suits you."

How close he was to truths left unspoken scared her to death. To distract him, she commented, "You, on the other hand, are thinner than you were. Harder. It's like all the excess has been stripped away and left just muscle and sinew and bone."

He sighed. "How true."

She laughed. "Never fear. I'll have you fattened back up in no time, Jack Spratt."

"Not if you work it all off of me making love." He kissed her then, adding, "By all means do your best to pack on the weight and take it right back off of me like this."

She shook her head in mock dismay. "I knew it. Sex and supper. That's all you want from me." The phrase "barefoot and pregnant in the kitchen" slid through her mind, but she cut the thought off in panic and prayed the same phrase hadn't occurred to him.

The humor bled out of his gaze until it was so black and so intense she could hardly bear to look at it. "Honey, sex and supper don't even scratch the surface of what I want from you tonight." His voice dropped to a husky whisper. "Tonight, I want it all."

And what about tomorrow?

He didn't bring it up, and she was vividly aware of the omission. He always had been a James Bond kind of guy. Love 'em and leave 'em. Apparently, two years in a box hadn't changed that about him. And two years hadn't changed her need for him, either. Hadn't diminished it one bit. Which meant she was left exactly where she was before, suspecting that they'd just have this short time together before he left her. Again. Could she survive that twice in one lifetime?

Truly, it was amazing that one of the scores of women left trailing in James Bond's wake never caught up with him and murdered him in bereavement or an excess of passion. Ian Fleming might have understood spies, but he sure as heck didn't understand women.

And then Jagger's hands closed on her body and all concern about anything beyond this exact moment flew away into the night.

Their lovemaking was achingly slow. Jagger seemed to want to savor every single second of it. A slight frown of concentration wrinkled his brow until she finally murmured, "You look so serious. Are you not enjoying yourself, or have you just forgotten what comes next?"

A snort of laughter escaped him. "I think I remember, thanks." He added more seriously, "I'll die remembering this moment with you."

"No talk of death tonight, okay?" she replied softly.

"You've got it. I'm alive. You're alive. Let's celebrate that."

And with that he wrapped her in his strong arms and rolled down the beach with her until the cold surf washed up on their feet. She squealed and he laughed, pulling her on top of him. Their laughter mingled as she looped her arms around his neck and gazed down at him with her heart in her eyes. The laughter drained out of his gaze until nothing was left but raw need that stole her breath away.

He whispered, "For a while there, I didn't think I was going to make it out of that box alive."

"But you did."

"It was a close thing. I was on the edge of breaking when you opened that door."

"But I did."

"I wasn't going to leave with you at first, you know. I thought it was a trick."

"I wouldn't have left you there, Jagger. I'd have found a way to get you out of that crate, even if I had to call in the National Guard."

"I doubt that rock is American soil, honey. But thanks for the thought."

She grinned down at him. "I always could

have messed with a cargo manifest and gotten your reefer unit off-loaded someplace and then conveniently lost track of."

He pushed her hair back and tucked it behind her ear. "My brave little innocent. AbaCo's goons would've caught you."

"I dunno. I'm pretty familiar with their computer systems. I know my way around most of their safeguards. And after all, I am Danger Girl."

He laughed quietly; then a speculative gleam entered his eyes. After a moment, he shook his head. "Later. I don't want to talk business right now."

Everything about their lovemaking was exactly as she remembered—but better. His hardness to her softness, his relentless energy, his finesse, his uncanny ability to know exactly what felt best to her as he stroked her with hand and mouth and body to a fever pitch. Bright lights exploded behind her eyelids, electric shocks zinged across her skin and orgasm after orgasm ripped through her.

She gasped his name, clinging to him as the

universe dissolved around her. Likewise, he buried his face against her neck and groaned as his body shuddered deep within hers.

Gradually, she became aware of dampness on her neck. "Jagger?" she asked.

He lifted his head to gaze down at her, and she was stunned to see tear tracks on his cheeks.

Right then, right there, her heart broke. It split wide open, its vulnerable interior exposed and raw. Then into the fissures flowed something warm and soothing, something entirely right. Love. For this man. This wonderful man who'd endured so much suffering and come out the other side of it able to give of himself, able to forgive.

She reached up and tenderly wiped away his tears.

He flashed her a crooked smile. "Guess I'm still a little messed up in the head."

"It's not messed up to shed a tear. You've been to hell and back. You're authorized to be a little emotional."

He took a deep breath. "It's real, isn't it? I'm

really free, aren't I? You're not going to make a phone call and have AbaCo's thugs swoop in and haul me back to my box, are you?"

She smiled at him and reached up to smooth the frown off his brow with her fingertips. "No, I'm not. And yes, Jagger. You're really free. I never would have helped them, particularly not with harming or kidnapping you. Nobody's coming to get you."

He stared at her for a long time as the truth of her words seemed to gradually sink in. Eventually, he shrugged. "We do still have the FBI to deal with. They may not be a walk in the park to convince that we're innocent."

Well, he was innocent. She hoped that the extenuating circumstances of saving a man's life would get her cleared of the charges against her, but it wasn't a guaranteed thing. She said bravely, "Once they hear your side of the story, they'll drop the charges against you."

"From your mouth to God's ear, eh?"

She gazed at every nuance of his expression as the worry slowly gave way to more hopeful thoughts. He had every reason to be cynical, she supposed. Everyone had abandoned him, believed him dead. Nobody had fought hard enough to find out how he'd died or to verify if it was even true.

Renewed guilt poured through her. Even she'd been willing to think the worst of him. "I'm sorry I didn't come looking for you sooner, Jagger."

He smiled down at her. "Don't worry about it. I'll be eternally grateful to you for getting me out of there."

"No, really—"

He laid two fingers across her mouth. "No, really. You're forgiven. It's fine."

He was a remarkable man. She didn't know if, in the same situation, she could find such generosity of spirit in herself. How on earth had she ever caught the attention of a man like him? She had to be the luckiest woman alive. She drank in the sight of him greedily. And that was probably why she noticed the faint frown that flitted through his eyes.

"What?" she murmured.

"It just occurred to me that we didn't use

any kind of protection just now. Lord knows I haven't been exposed to any diseases in the past two years, but we still should've taken precautions against a preg—"

He broke off.

Panic erupted in her gut, clawing at her ribs. She held her breath, hoping against hope that she wasn't reading the memory in his eyes correctly. But she knew she was.

"When I was sick…" he started.

Oh, God.

"You said something to me. Something about…" He frowned as if struggling to retrieve the memory.

Please, please let him fail.

Triumph flashed in his gaze. "A baby—"

A thunderous frown gathered on his brow. He lurched upright, staring down at her in mingled disbelief and fury. "*Our* baby."

Still she said nothing. He hadn't actually asked her a question, after all.

His voice was terrible in its piano-wire-tight restraint. "Is that true? Do we have a child? Or did you just say that to get me to fight to live?"

It would be so easy to take the out he'd offered her. To let the glib lie roll off her tongue. Yeah, sure. That was it. She'd lied about a kid to make him fight to live. Except she had a responsibility to her daughter. To their daughter. And at the end of the day, she had a responsibility to him, too. He had a right to know.

She sighed. Took a deep breath. Said a mental goodbye to their great connection and happily-ever-after future. And answered, "It's true. Her name is Michelle and she's fifteen months old. Lest you wonder whether or not she's yours, a, I hadn't been with anyone else in over a year, and, b, you only have to take one look at her to know. She's the spitting image of you. But if you want to do a paternity test on her, I'll consent to it."

Jagger jerked away from her, taking his warmth and safety with him. He sat in the sand with his back partially turned to her, his shoulders hunched, his usual restlessness completely absent. He stared at the ocean for a long time and then shifted his gaze to the thick dusting of stars overhead. But still he said nothing. The silence was deafening.

He'd shut her out. Drawn away from her totally. No part of him was open to her. It was as if she didn't exist, and the love they'd just made had never happened. In an instant, he was a stranger to her.

The loss was devastating. As bad as losing him before had been, this was a hundred times worse. He'd left her again, and yet he was sitting a foot away from her. She'd thought his physical disappearance made her feel abandoned. *Now* she knew the true meaning of the word.

She felt an odd and painful ache in her chest. Oh, wait. That was her heart shriveling and turning to dust. Slowly, she pulled herself upright. Hugging her knees, she cautiously glanced over at him. What was there to say?

In a small voice, she murmured, "I'd have told you right away if I had known how to get in touch with you."

"Did you continue with the pregnancy because you object to abortion?"

"Good Lord, no! I kept her because I wanted her. I wanted your—our—child. She's the greatest kid ever! Wait until you meet her—" She broke off abruptly. "If you want to meet her, of course. I don't expect you to dive into parenthood just because she exists. It's your choice…"

She trailed off as he stared at her blankly. She couldn't read anything at all in that flat gaze. Until he gave her some indication of his reaction, she didn't dare say more at all.

He stared at her for a long time. Four hundred sixty-two seconds. She counted each one. And then he said neutrally, "Of course AbaCo knows about Michelle. You're on the company's health care plan, no doubt."

"Not to mention I've taken her into the office from time to time for company parties."

"Do they know she's mine?"

"Truly, Jagger, to look at her is to know she's yours. She's a tiny, female version of you. The resemblance is startling." A cold chill was spreading through her. When she'd found out the FBI wanted her, she'd known better than to contact her mother by phone or e-mail. She'd just assumed, though, that Jagger would make it all better. But the way he was frowning right now was alarming in the extreme.

He swore violently under his breath. Then he spoke urgently, his voice hard. Tight. "We've got to call Don to come get us. We need to fly out of here as soon as possible. Tonight if he can swing it."

Horror exploded in her chest. "Are you leaving me when we get to the big island, then?"

His gaze snapped to her. "No, of course not. You're coming with me. But we've got to go get Michelle before AbaCo does. Hell, they've had nearly a week to snatch her." He pushed a distracted hand through his hair and muttered, "Cripes. I didn't need a liability like this for them to use to get their hooks back into me."

Ohgod, ohgod, ohgod.

He swore under his breath some more as he sat up, continuing to mutter that AbaCo's goons were too smart to miss this opportunity to kidnap an exploitable asset like a child and that they no doubt had her by now.

Emily jumped to her feet in terror. "They have Michelle?" she cried frantically. "Come on! We've got to go!" She wrung her hands in impatience as Jagger continued to sit in the sand.

"Honey, a few minutes or hours now isn't going to matter. If they connected you to my escape, AbaCo's men showed up at your house within twenty-four hours. In that case, they've had the child for days, by now. If we're lucky, they haven't made the connection yet and she's still safe."

Emily frowned. "But she's not at my house. My mother took her back to the mainland for the holidays."

Interest lit Jagger's eyes. "Where is she now?"

"With my mother's family in Virginia."

"Do they have the same last name as you?"

"No. My mother remarried after my father died and took his name. His family is Andersons, not Grainger."

"Hmm. Maybe there's a chance then that AbaCo doesn't know where to find her. We need to get you to a phone so you can call your mother and warn her not to open the door for any strangers until we get there. If AbaCo gets a hold of your daughter, they'll use her to leverage the two of us into doing exactly what they want."

Relief flooded Emily that AbaCo probably didn't have Michelle yet. But then visions of Jagger's tiny prison flashed through her mind and a new wave of panic broke over her. Her baby couldn't end up like that! She just couldn't.

"Breathe, Em. We'll get to her first."

She took several deep breaths. It would be okay. Michelle would be safe. She had to be. Any other possibility was simply unthinkable. The two of them quickly hunted down their clothes and she pulled hers back on, oblivious of the sand now grating uncomfortably against her skin.

As they walked quickly back to the cabin, her mind finally began to function again, even if all it did was jump from one disjointed thought to another. At least it did until one odd observation registered and then stuck in her craw.

It grew into something uncomfortable smoldering in her gut. It wasn't anger exactly, but it was irritating, and she didn't know exactly how to react.

Jagger still hadn't said a word about how he felt about finding out that he was a father. Okay, she'd grant that it was a shock and might take some getting used to before he figured out how he felt. But so far he'd called Michelle a liability, an exploitable asset and leverage. Oh, and once he'd referred to Michelle as *her* daughter. Not his.

She tried to argue herself out of it. She'd determined a long time ago not to force parenthood on Jagger if she ever found him. She'd made the decision on her own to go through with the pregnancy and to be a single parent. She'd vowed to have no expectations of him.

But her jaw couldn't help but tighten at the way he'd labeled her precious daughter like some sort of inconvenient object to be managed.

Something else Ian Fleming had never bothered to reveal about James Bond—although in fairness to the author, she probably should have known it herself—he was lousy father material.

Chapter 11

A baby. Holy smokes.

Jagger stared out the window of the Boeing 777 at the featureless blue of the Pacific Ocean passing below. They'd land in Los Angeles in an hour, and then, assuming nothing went wrong, they'd be on their way to Virginia. And his *daughter.*

The concept still blew his mind, and he'd had nearly twelve hours to get used to it while Don flew to Lyle's island from Honolulu, took them back to Oahu and then they boarded this flight to the mainland. Most men got seven or eight months to adapt to the idea of being a father, lucky bastards. And based on the degree of shock he was currently experiencing, they needed all eight months, too.

Even in the low-quality home photos of the toddler that Emily had shown him, Michelle did look startlingly like him. There really wasn't any question that the child was his. And besides, Emily wasn't the kind of woman to lie about something like this. If she said Michelle was his daughter, then it was true.

He'd never even met the child, and already he could hardly sit still in his seat as he pondered the possibilities if AbaCo managed to get a hold of her. What was up with that? It was as if he'd gone from zero to protective Daddy in ten seconds flat.

He'd listened in a state of wonder approaching disbelief as Emily eagerly regaled him with two years' worth of accumulated stories about her pregnancy, birth and raising of Michelle to date. She sounded like a cute little kid—curious and cheerful and bright. But his? Whoa.

Maybe if he could get past his horror at the idea of AbaCo kidnapping a tiny child and taking her from her mother—and father—he'd be joyful at the news that he had a daughter. But instead, panic rose up to all but choke him every time he relaxed his mental guard for even a second. He didn't have time to celebrate the news. He had to keep Michelle safe—hell, keep her alive—first. And knowing AbaCo, that was going to take every ounce of his skill and commitment.

As for Emily, he had to give her credit. She was a great mom if her frantic need to protect her child was any indication. She hadn't slept a wink last night after his revelation that Michelle might be in danger. Thankfully, she'd dropped off in her seat beside him about an hour ago from sheer emotional exhaustion.

Which was a good thing. He wasn't sure he could take much more of the sudden tension that had sprung up between them. She'd done her best to mask it, but it was clear she was annoyed with him for not showing a little more reaction—good or bad—to parenthood.

But how could he? He had to focus all his energy on saving Michelle, to keep his mind firmly on the task at hand, which was to reach

Michelle and secure the child before AbaCo found her. He'd have time to figure out how he felt about being a father later.

He closed his eyes. Tried to catch a nap before they landed. But it was no use. He'd slept too much over the past week of recuperation, and frankly he was too wired with anxiety to sleep now. He occupied the remainder of the flight imagining possible scenarios when they landed that ranged from smooth sailing to their next flight to an armed party of AbaCo operatives jumping them in the terminal.

In his line of work, it was all about contingency planning. About having a plan B for every situation that could possibly present itself to a covert operative like him. Then it was a simple matter of him assessing the situation and activating the appropriate response plan. No sweat, right? He'd done it a hundred times before. So why was he sitting here sweating bullets?

It could only be the parenthood wild card. Being a father had done something weird to his gut. Something at a subliminal level that he had no control of. It was as if some violently protective switch had been flipped on toward this small person who looked so much like him.

Under other circumstances, normal circumstances, he'd have relished these new feelings. But at the moment, jitters all but rattled him out of his seat and his mind was a jumbled mess. How was he going to save anybody in this frame of mind? He had to get control of himself! Even resorting to meditation failed him in the end.

He couldn't imagine how Emily was holding it together at all. She had a two-year head start on him in loving Michelle. Plus, there was that whole mother-bear-protecting-threatened-cub instinct for Emily to deal with.

When the plane bumped onto the runway at LAX, he was relieved as Emily blinked awake to reveal grim determination in her gaze and no hint of panic. Thank goodness. He didn't need a hysterical mother on his hands.

They had no bags to collect and he rushed Emily through the terminal at nearly a run, keeping a sharp eye out for any pursuers. Their quick pace would force any small surveillance team to scramble and reveal themselves to a trained operative like him. Sure enough, as they approached the gate for their flight to Washington, D.C., he thought he spotted a furtive movement out of the corner of his eye. He cursed under his breath and Emily went stiff beside him.

"Keep moving," he muttered. "Don't give any indication that we've just passed our gate." Her head started to turn and he bit out, "Don't look around."

Her head snapped forward.

He murmured, "We're gonna have to lose the tail before we can board our flight. Just do what I tell you to and be prepared to move fast. Got it?"

"Yes." She sounded on the verge of throwing up.

"Be strong, Em. For Michelle. Be Danger Girl."

Her shoulders squared beside him. *Good girl. Or more accurately, brave Mom.*

He proceeded to weave through the terminal, ducking through stores, reversing course abruptly and generally being a pain in the ass to follow. A couple of times he spotted AbaCo operatives dodging out of his line of sight. It looked like a three-man team. Not nearly enough to stay on a guy like him who'd figured out that he was being tailed. At least the team wasn't trying to move in and snatch him and Emily. Not yet. Not in this public a place with the amount of security major airports boasted these days.

For her part, Emily was a trouper, never complaining as he dragged her around like a rag doll.

He carefully eyed the high-quality diving watch Lyle had given him. He'd have to time this practically down to the second.

One more loop through a crowded newsstand, and then it was time.

"C'mon," he bit out under his breath. He and Emily took off running at a dead sprint through the terminal. Agony speared through his side and he prayed he hadn't opened up the wounds.

But he didn't slow down. As they neared their gate, the final boarding call for their flight was being announced for the last time. Two gates prior to theirs, he yanked Emily down beside him, ducking below the levels of the chairs in the waiting areas. Crouched uncomfortably, the two of them duckwalked the last few yards to their gate.

The gate agent looked alarmed as they knelt guiltily before her ticket reader, and Jagger shot her his most charming smile past the fire searing in his side. "This is my girlfriend. My soon-to-be ex-wife and her lawyer are here, looking for us."

Sudden understanding lit the agent's face, and she obligingly whisked them onto the jet bridge and closed the door behind them.

"Your girlfriend?" Emily complained as they rushed toward the jet.

"Well, it's true, isn't it?"

That seemed to give her pause. At least it rendered her silent until they dropped into their seats, panting, and the plane had taken off. But he had faith he hadn't heard the last of it yet.

He was right.

"Look, Jagger. I never intended for Michelle to be your responsibility. I made the decision to have her and raise her by myself. You're under no obligation to get involved in her life as a parent. I don't expect it of you. You don't have to have anything to do with either one of us if you don't want to."

Irritation stabbed him and his voice was sharp as he muttered back, "You don't have a very high opinion of me, do you?"

She scowled. "I'm just saying I don't neces- sarily expect you to dive in and embrace the whole daddy thing. I won't even ask for child support. I'm doing fine on my own. Well, I was until I lost my job with AbaCo." She added hastily, "Not that it's any great loss. I couldn't work for a company like that in good con- science knowing what I do now about it. Your kidnapping was the final straw."

He turned to look her full in the face. "You mean there were other straws? What all *do* you know about them?"

"Quite a bit, actually."

Under the roar of the jet engines he asked quietly, "Do you know anything about illegal shipments they're making?"

She frowned. "I know stuff like the fact that most of the senior managers in my department worked together in the Stasi."

That shot both his brows sky-high. His mind raced. The Stasi had been the notorious secret police fist of the East German socialist regime. When East Germany had dissolved, so had the Stasi, thrusting thousands of trained covert operatives and thugs onto the street without jobs and without pensions. It had been a no-brainer that they'd turn en masse to crime. Like the KGB, which had become the core of the modern Russian mob, former Stasi agents formed the core of today's German Mafia. Was the *entire* shipping company an elaborate front for a crime syndicate?

Emily was speaking again. "The thing I can't understand is why they held you prisoner for two years. Why didn't they release you or just kill you?"

He laughed without humor. "I figured that

one out a long time ago. They were trying to brainwash me. To break my mind and then re-program me into a double agent to work for them."

Alarm shot across her face. "Did they suc-ceed?"

He snorted. "Nope." He paused and then added grimly, "And I've got you to thank for that. I was so fixated on my fury at you that all their efforts to crack me failed. I was too focused for their methods to work."

She winced. "So because you hated me, you were immune?"

He shrugged. "Yeah, pretty much."

"I wish I had known earlier. Found some way to save you."

He wasn't crazy about spending two years in a box and being beaten up and half starved. But it wasn't as though he could change that fact at this point. It was water under the bridge. And right now he needed to focus all his energy on reaching Michelle and making her safe. He also needed Emily completely focused on the job ahead.

He murmured soothingly, "What's done is done, Em."

She subsided but continued to look troubled.

Both of them slept for most of the transcontinental flight to Washington, D.C. He woke up when they began their descent. He had to assume AbaCo's thugs would have figured out by now where they'd flown off to and that a welcoming committee of some kind would be waiting to greet them. A welcoming committee he'd have to lose, and fast.

Before he and Emily could approach Michelle, he had to make absolutely sure they weren't being followed. He dared not lead AbaCo's men anywhere near the child. But by the same token, he doubted Emily would put up with much fooling around before she was reunited with her daughter. She might be acting fairly controlled, but he knew her well enough to know that she was pretty freaked out.

Once they landed he planned to make contact with his headquarters. He had no intention of turning himself in now, but he had to keep the lines of communication open, to make it clear that he was going to cooperate with the government, and start planting seeds of the idea that he and Emily might have been set up and might just have some fascinating facts of their own to reveal about their accusers.

If nothing else, Uncle Sam was gonna love picking Emily's brains for what she could reveal about AbaCo's "sensitive cargoes." The U.S. had suspected for a long time that elements within AbaCo were engaged in extensive international mob activity. But nobody had ever dreamed that the entire company might be a mob front. He feared that the missing agents who'd been sent in to infiltrate AbaCo before him had met a fate similar to or worse than his. He didn't know if he hoped they were still alive, or if, after all this time, they'd died and been put out of their misery. How long could any man stay sane living in a box?

Hopefully, with what Emily knew, maybe the U.S. government could build a case against the shipping giant that would stick. It was worth risking jail for. If they could bring down

AbaCo, their daughter would be safe once and for all. And that was worth *anything*.

First he and Emily had to get Michelle safely in their custody. Then they'd deal with the charges against them and take apart AbaCo once and for all.

They hadn't had time during the frantic run through LAX to call Emily's mother to check and make sure Michelle was safe, and he could only hope the woman had gotten Emily's single urgent e-mail to lock the doors and keep Michelle inside until Emily arrived to explain everything.

Their flight landed at Dulles International Airport and he didn't lead Emily through any evasive measures after they disembarked. In fact, he went out of his way to act unconcerned, as if he believed they'd lost their tail in Los Angeles. He made no effort even to check for tails. In the first place, he'd be an idiot to assume anything other than they were being followed. And in the second place, he wouldn't be able to lose the tail anyway until he and Emily had picked up their rental car and hit the road. Besides, he *felt* the tail behind him. Hell, he almost smelled sauerkraut in the air.

He supposed it was technically possible that this was just paranoia and irrational fear for Michelle's safety kicking in. But he doubted it. Either way, it didn't make any difference in how he behaved. He stopped at a kiosk and bought an outrageously overpriced cell phone and a bunch of prepaid minutes, then calmly guided her through Dulles toward the rental car counter.

Emily incorrectly interpreted his calm to mean they were in the clear, and she relaxed accordingly. Which suited his purposes just fine. He didn't disabuse her of the notion that they were safe. She needed the break from her continuous panic of the past twenty-four hours.

He drove when they left the airport. He had a sinking feeling that his specialized offensive driving skills were going to be called upon before this day was over. He pointed the car south out of the airport, winding along back roads southward into Virginia.

"So where exactly are your mother and Michelle in Virginia?" he queried once they were well away from the airport. "Can you find it on the map the car agent gave us and show me?"

"Sure. They're in Chestnut Grove." She fumbled with the map for a minute, then pointed at a speck in the Shenandoah Valley, right in the heart of Virginia horse country.

"We'll stop at the next gas station and get a more detailed map of the state. I'll need you to find three or four different routes to reach Chestnut Grove."

She frowned. "Are you expecting trouble?"

He replied with false levity, "Better safe than sorry, Danger Girl."

Over the next half hour, he had no luck spotting the AbaCo tail. And that worried him. He went so far as to guide the car onto a highway and push the speed up to twenty miles per hour over the speed limit for a few minutes. Nobody matched their speed behind him. Swearing under his breath, he pulled over at the first rest stop they came to. The lack of a visible tail could mean only one thing.

He sent Emily inside to buy snacks for them. Once she was out of sight, he commenced examining the car in detail to check for an electronic tracking device. It was the only explanation. AbaCo's men were hanging back out of visual range and using a radio to follow them.

He wasn't at all surprised to find the small black disk magnetically attached to the top side of the muffler of their car. It was very well hidden. Professionally, in fact. But unfortunately for AbaCo, he was a pro, too.

With the transmitter in his pocket, he strolled into the rest stop to join Emily. It was an easy enough matter to find out that the college student in the line in front of them for hamburgers was headed to Richmond. When the kid laid the keys to his rental car on the counter to pay for his food, it was even easier for Jagger to read the make, model and license plate number of the kid's car off the key tag.

While Emily ducked into a restroom, Jagger strolled outside and attached the tracking device to the underside of the kid's rear bumper before the student pulled out of the truck stop.

Jagger timed their departure so they actually followed the kid for a few miles, just in case the AbaCo tails had closed in to visual range while he and Emily had been stopped. Once AbaCo saw their car moving in the same direction as the tracking beacon, the goons would back out of visual range again. And the fact that they were following the wrong car hopefully wouldn't dawn on them until the student had arrived in Richmond several hours from now—long after Jagger and Emily had disappeared into the rural back roads of the Shenandoah Valley.

Jagger drove erratically, speeding up and slowing down, slamming on the brakes and making last-second turns, and even pounded down a few dusty dirt roads. No plumes of dust kicked up behind them. Eventually, he became convinced that no one was following them, at close range or otherwise.

He held out a hand across the car to Emily. "I need the cell phone."

"The phone! I'm so used to being on the Rock and not having one I forgot we had it. Let me call my mother—"

He cut her off gently. "Me first. Please. It's important."

"Uh. Oh. Okay. Here."

He dialed with one hand and held the device up to his ear. A marine clerk answered the line.

"This is Captain Holtz. I need to speak to—"

He got no further with the clerk. The familiar voice of his boss came on the line. "Jagger. Damn I'm glad to hear your voice again. Thought we'd lost you there, for a while. Where are you?"

"Not far away, actually."

"That's excellent news. You're still planning to turn yourself in, right? Do you have the woman with you?"

He glanced over at Emily. "Yes to both."

"Come in ASAP. The sooner we get statements from you, the sooner we can sort this mess out and clear your name."

"Right. About that. I've got some good news and some bad news for you, sir. The good news is that between the two of us, Miss Grainger and I should be able to hand you enough information to bury AbaCo once and for all. The bad news is we have something else to take care of first. We can't turn ourselves in just yet."

"Jagger." The colonel's warning tone was grim. "If you run around like a fugitive, the credibility of your entire story will be called into doubt. Your only shot at clearing yourself is to get your butt in here now."

Jagger winced. "Sir, I know you're right. Nonetheless, I have to take care of this problem first. It's not negotiable. You can tell the FBI that I'll be in touch with them in a few days."

"How many days?" the colonel demanded.

"As many days as it takes, sir. We'll come in, I swear. Just not yet."

"You're putting me in an awkward situation, son."

A heavy silence fell between them. There was nothing more for Jagger to say. His daughter came first. Before his career, before his safety, before his *life*. But then inspiration struck. "Could you do me a favor, sir?"

A harrumph rumbled in his ear. "What kind of favor?"

"Broker a deal for me. If the FBI will help me take care of this personal problem of mine first, I'll turn myself in and cooperate fully with them when it's successfully resolved. I'm not exaggerating when I say we can bury AbaCo. Turns out the entire company is a front for German Mafia activity."

The colonel went dead silent. Jagger heard the guy's mental wheels turning fast. "That's pretty tempting bait. The entire company, you say? But the firm's worth billions. If we took that out, we'd financially gut the German Mafia. Crime in Europe would plummet. Countries all over the world would owe us big time…" His voice trailed off. "I could work with that."

Jagger held his breath. This might be just the break they needed. With the full resources of the FBI to help them, AbaCo wouldn't stand a chance of getting its mitts on Michelle.

"It may take me a day or two to work this deal, Jagger. You gonna be okay in the meantime?"

"Yes, sir. We'll be lying low and taking care of business."

"I'll do what I can. But if they turn down your offer, they're gonna come after you hard. They're pissed that an operative of your experience turned on them."

"I didn't turn, sir." The colonel said nothing in response, and Jagger added a little desperately, "C'mon. You know me better than that."

"Yeah. I guess I do. Either way, be quick about your business."

"I hear you loud and clear, sir. And thank you."

A snort. "Don't thank me. If you want to cover my ass and yours, turn yourself in."

Jagger disconnected the call thoughtfully. Problem was, once the colonel found out that he and Emily had a child together, all hell was going to break loose anyway. Government operatives were emphatically not supposed to become romantically involved with their informants or human assets. By using her to gain entrance to the AbaCo party, he had cast Emily in the role of an agent, albeit unwitting, of the U.S. government. Still, it was enough of a professional entanglement that she was entirely off-limits to him romantically. It was going to be just a wee bit difficult to get around the fact that they had a daughter whose age placed her conception firmly on that New Year's Eve two years ago when Jagger had used Emily on a mission.

He was screwed either way. That being the case, he might as well save Michelle and unite Emily with her daughter before he went down in flames.

Grimly, he handed the phone to Emily. "Don't give your mom any details over the phone. Just tell her to stay inside with other members of your family, don't open the door to any strangers, and for God's sake, don't let Michelle out of her sight for an instant."

Emily nodded and made the call. Even across the car, Jagger heard Mrs. Anderson's agitation at the other end of the line. Apparently, the danger of the situation had been adequately conveyed and understood. Good. The way he figured it, a grandma was a mommy once removed, which made a grandmother almost as deadly as a mother when her grandchild was threatened.

"How much longer?" Emily murmured as she put away her phone.

"An hour."

It was a tense sixty minutes. He fought his urge to stand on the accelerator and barely managed to hold the car somewhere close to the speed limit. The more time he had to process the idea of having a child, the more connected he felt to her—and he'd never even met Michelle! It bordered on bizarre.

His anxiety climbed with every mile closer they came to her. He was about to meet his daughter. A human being that he'd helped create. The enormity of it overwhelmed him.

What would Michelle think of him? Would she be scared of the grim stranger with her eyes? Would she instinctively recognize him and cut him a break? What did a person do with a fifteen-month-old, anyway? Was that too old for peekaboo? Should he have tried to find her a toy in that rest stop? What did kids that age play with, anyway?

He checked his rampant nerves sharply. She was a baby, for crying out loud. She wouldn't quiz him on his qualifications to be a parent, thank God, because he was grossly unprepared. The brain freeze induced by the mere thought of facing a diaper or a bath was proof enough of that.

"Are you okay?" Emily asked him abruptly.

He started. "Why do you ask?"

"You look about ready to throw up."

He grimaced. "Impending parenthood does that to a guy." He knew the words were a mistake the moment they left his mouth.

Emily's face went closed, and she turned to stare out the passenger window, hurt written in the lines of her neck and shoulders.

"I didn't mean it like that, Em. I'm just nervous. I want Michelle to like me." He took a deep breath and confessed, "I don't know the first thing about kids."

"Neither did I. But you'll catch on fast enough. That is, if you feel like sticking around."

He huffed. "Of course I'll be sticking around. I have every intention of stepping up to my new responsibilities."

Emily flinched again. What had he said now? He was looking forward to becoming a dad. Eager to change the subject, he said, "When we reach your uncle's house, I'll stay outside and make sure we don't have any company while you go in and get Michelle."

She started. "What? I thought we were going to stay with my aunt and uncle for a while."

He frowned. "Of course not. We've got to get away from anywhere AbaCo might look for the child."

Skepticism dripped in her voice. "So you're going to…what? Run around acting like a superspy with a toddler in tow?"

That *had* been his plan. Although when she put it like that… "Have you got a better idea?"

"Well, no. But I don't think that's much of a plan. Little kids are pretty high maintenance, and it's not like you can strap her into her car seat for hours on end, stick a bottle in her mouth and call it good."

Damn.

Emily must've read his mind because she snorted. "She's not a newborn. She sleeps about ten hours at night and takes either one long or two short naps each day. The rest of the time she's busy climbing and exploring and generally destroying everything she can lay her hands on."

Oh, Lord. The weapons and delicate electronics that were part and parcel of his job being pawed by a toddler—yikes. Time for a new plan.

He blurted, "Do you know anybody in Virginia who's an old friend? Somebody you haven't contacted in years? Like not since you worked for AbaCo?"

"No. Nobody. Just my mom's family."

"How about your mother or your aunt and

uncle? Would they know someone who'd take you and Michelle in?"

"What? And bring AbaCo's thugs to their doorstep? I can't do that to a family friend, or to someone I've never met for that matter!"

As a trained operative, he didn't hesitate to use anyone and everyone around him to accomplish a mission. And frankly, now wasn't the time to stand on ethics. It was time to marshal whatever resources they could and use them, no matter what the risks to others. "Em—"

She must have heard the lecture coming in his voice because she waved it off. "I don't want to hear it. It's bad enough that Michelle and I are in potential danger. I won't do that to anyone else. Find a way to keep us safe without involving other people."

"I'm not superhuman," he snapped.

"I don't know. From what I've seen of you so far, you come pretty close. Not many people could've survived what you have. And certainly not with their minds and bodies and souls intact."

In an attempt to lighten the mood he reminded her, "Hey, you're Danger Girl, not me. I'm just some guy, remember?"

"No, you're Super Spy. You're not just some guy."

"Danger Girl and Super Spy. We make some pair, huh?"

She wasn't about to be derailed so easily, however. "You've come through stuff intact that would have killed other people. You can do this, Jagger. I know it."

He wasn't sure anything about him was intact. "Then you've got to let me do what I know how to do, the way I know how to do it. Don't fight me on this. We need to take Michelle and get her away from anyone that AbaCo might somehow connect to the two of you. They know we're in the Washington, D.C., area, and they'll scour your records for any contacts in this part of the country. Your entire family is at risk as long as we're with them. Likewise, they'll be watching every hotel, restaurant, bus station, you name it. We can't go anywhere public. We've got to go to ground."

She stared at him. Hard. He avoided meeting her gaze under the guise of watching the road.

She huffed. "Fine. We'll do it your way. But you get to tell my mother."

Chapter 12

Emily didn't wait for Jagger to get out of the car. She raced for the front door, which opened without her having to ring the bell. "Michelle!" she cried.

"Mamaaa!"

Her relief when that sturdy, beloved little body rushed into her arms spilled down Emily's cheeks unchecked in hot, wet tracks. She buried her face in her daughter's silky curls. Out of the corner of her eye, she just caught a glimpse of the shotgun her stepfather leaned inside the door before he followed his granddaughter outside. Good. They'd taken her warning seriously.

"Mama?" Michelle frowned up at her,

as if unsure whether or not she should be crying, too.

"I'm crying because I'm happy, sweetheart. I missed you, munchkin. Did you miss me?"

The little girl reached up to touch Emily's damp cheeks. Then she smiled and wriggled free, eager to be on the go once more. Emily laughed. "Hold on a second, sweetie. There's someone I want you to meet."

She scooped up Michelle before she could take off like the world's cutest bullet, and turned.

Jagger was standing beside the car. His face was devoid of expression, but he stood absolutely still, his intense gaze riveted on his daughter. Something about him must have captured his daughter's attention, too, for she stuck a thumb in her mouth and stared back, her own restless nature, so much like her father's, curbed for the moment.

"This is my friend Jagger. Jagger, this is Michelle."

He moved then, easing forward cautiously. He stuck a finger out and touched one of the child's bouncy curls carefully. Michelle made a fast grab and captured his finger, promptly stuffing it into her mouth.

A look of wonder spread across Jagger's face as she gnawed enthusiastically on his fingertip.

"Teething," Emily murmured apologetically. "Sorry."

"That's entirely all right," he murmured back.

Her mother's voice startled her from the front door. She'd completely forgotten about her mom in the magic of the moment. "Who's your friend, Emily? Aren't you going to introduce us?"

"Oh. Sorry, Mom. This is Jagger Holtz. Jagger, my mother. Doris Anderson."

He nodded gravely. "It's a pleasure to meet you, ma'am."

Her mother's shrewd gaze flitted back and forth between Michelle and Jagger and comprehension dawned. Emily winced. So much for that cat. One look at Michelle and Jagger side by side, and the feline was irrevocably out of the bag as to who was Michelle's father.

Thankfully, Doris merely pursed her lips and said nothing.

Emily's stepfather boomed, "Well, come on in and sit a spell."

She looked over her shoulder at Jagger. "That's Al. I told you about him. He's my mother's husband."

"Handy with a shotgun, I see," Jagger muttered.

Emily grinned. "Oh, yeah. Terrorized the few dates I managed to land in high school."

Jagger grinned. "Stupid boys. Didn't know what they were missing when they let you get away. You're worth braving howitzers over, let alone a measly shotgun."

She smiled into Michelle's hair as they went inside. She turned the toddler loose within the confines of four walls and watched until the toddler raced out of sight. She spoke briskly to her mother. "We need to pack up a few of Michelle's things. Jagger and I need to leave with her right away."

Thunder landed on her mother's brow. "I don't think it's a good idea to go haring off all over the countryside with a baby in tow, young lady—"

"Don't young lady me, Mom. Some really dangerous people are after us."

"All the more reason not to go running around."

She'd feared her mother might be obstinate about this. "Jagger knows what he's doing. He can handle the people who are chasing us. He just needs to know that Michelle is safe and that she won't be used to get to us."

"She won't be if she stays here. Al's brothers are hunters, too. They all know their way around a gun if it comes to it."

Emily sighed. "We're not talking about a handful of bubbas with shotguns here. These men are ex-Stasi agents. They're mobsters. Violent criminals."

"So call the police and let them deal with this." Ever practical, Doris was.

Emily glanced over at Jagger. "Help me out, here."

He spoke quietly. "Think of a team of Special Forces commandos storming your home and killing everyone in the place so they can grab Michelle. They'll come in all at once through the windows and doors, toting submachine guns that shoot through your walls like tissue paper. They'll attack at night using night-vision goggles and you'll be completely blind. Not that Al or his brothers will get a shot off at them anyway before the team mows them down like sheep. Their weapons will literally cut you in half with bullets."

Everyone in the room stared at Jagger, aghast.

"Who are you?" Al finally asked.

"I'm a covert operative trained in the same methods as the people who are coming after Michelle. The assault I just described is what I'd do in the same situation. These guys are professionals. They're armed to the teeth and they're ruthless. With all due respect, sir, you and your family are no match for them."

Doris spoke up tartly. "Sounds like you're no match for them by yourself, either."

He smiled ruefully at her. "I'm not. That's why Emily and I have to leave and take Michelle someplace where we can hide until the authorities catch up with these guys."

Al grunted. "So surround the house with police or FBI or whoever."

Emily winced. "Right, well, there's a problem with that. Jagger and I have had a little misunderstanding with the FBI and they've got federal warrants out for our arrest. We'll be able to clear up most of the charges as soon as we talk to them, but first we have to make sure that Michelle's safe. That's why we need to take her and leave."

Doris announced firmly, "You're not going anywhere until both of you get a decent meal into you. You look half-dead with exhaustion."

A hot meal was Doris's cure-all for everything that ailed a person. Emily sighed. She looked over at Jagger for approval. He nodded reluctantly and she turned back to her mom. "All right. We'll stay for supper. But then we'll have to go."

Rather than argue anymore with her mother, Emily headed for Michelle's room and began to pack clothes, diapers and toys for her daughter. Doris stomped up and down the hall and did a lot of mumbling under her breath but did not interfere. Emily was relieved to be left to pack in peace.

Over the course of the next hour, however, a repeat of the initial argument occurred, first between her and Al, and then between her and Jagger against everyone again. In the end, Jagger reluctantly agreed to stay at the house until he and Emily had someplace specific in mind to head for.

But over the meal, Jagger recruited Al's family to help him find someplace to go. He laid out his requirements succinctly. They needed someplace isolated to hole up with Michelle where the FBI could eventually come and interview him. That place needed to be free of any family or friends of Emily's, Doris's or Al's that AbaCo could track down. It needed to be reasonably close to Washington, D.C., and it needed to not be connected to any commercially traceable databases, like those used by hotels or stores.

Doris frowned. "In other words, you need to

find the home of a complete stranger who will take you in despite the fact that you bring life-threatening risk with you."

Jagger grimaced. "Pretty much."

Emily's mother excused herself from the table. "I may know just the person, and now's the perfect time to catch her."

Emily and Jagger cleared the table and started washing and drying the dishes while her mother signed on to the computer in the dining room. Doris was online a total of maybe two minutes, and then she marched into the kitchen, smiling broadly.

"I've found a place for you three to stay. However, I'm not telling you where it is unless you agree to take me with you."

Emily groaned. Jagger cocked an eyebrow and commented wryly, "I see where you get your stubborn streak from, Em."

"Well?" Doris demanded belligerently. "You'll need a babysitter if you plan on running all over creation, and I'm not letting that baby out of my sight until I know she's safe."

Jagger shrugged. "You have a point. Emily

and I may be a bit occupied over the next several days with security arrangements and after that with debriefings."

Yeah, and going to jail if the FBI didn't buy their respective stories about AbaCo. In that event, Doris would need to be nearby to take custody of Michelle. Emily glanced over at Jagger and saw the exact same thought mirrored in his troubled gaze.

Her mother beamed. "I'm already packed." When Emily scowled, her mother continued. "I did it while you were packing Michelle's things." She added defiantly, "I won't be any trouble."

"Right, Mom. No trouble at all. Now I've got you to worry about, too."

Doris shrugged. "Take it or leave it. I go, too, or I don't give up the location to you."

Emily looked over at Jagger. He said in resignation, "All right. You go, too, Doris. Two mother bears protecting the cub has to be better than one."

Once the decision was made, they left almost immediately. There was a brief flap when

Jagger refused to let Doris tell Al where they were going. But when Jagger gently suggested that if Al was captured and tortured for the information it would be best if the older man didn't, in fact, know where Jagger, Emily and Michelle were, everyone subsided in horror.

Thankfully, in anticipation of picking up Michelle and a bunch of baby gear, Jagger had rented a full-sized car. They set out into the night.

"So who are we going to visit?" Jagger asked after about a half hour of evasive driving designed to make sure they had no tail.

Doris replied, "I belong to an online chat group for single moms and the occasional grandma. One of the moms lives in this general area. When I went online and asked if she'd mind a few houseguests, she invited us right away."

Emily asked sharply, "Does she understand the risk in taking us in?"

"I made it clear there were some legal problems and that Michelle's safety was an issue. I wasn't sure how much I should explain over a computer, though."

Jagger nodded. "You did well to keep it vague. We'll fill in our hostess when we arrive and she can decide if she wants us to stay or not."

Emily murmured, "Can't we just drive to Washington, D.C., and walk into FBI head-quarters tonight?"

Jagger frowned. "In the first place, I have every reason to believe AbaCo's men will be staking out the place. I doubt we'd make it anywhere near downtown D.C. before they snatched us.

"In the second place, I want to bag these bas-tards once and for all. The only bait we know for sure that AbaCo will bite at is me and you. As soon as you and I give our statements to a federal attorney or two, we'll have all the backup we need. Then we show ourselves to AbaCo's goons, they make a grab for us and Uncle Sam grabs the lot of them. A couple of days. Maybe a week. And then this will all be over."

It sounded so easy. If only she could believe it would work out like that.

Jagger drove grimly into the night. His plan sounded straightforward enough. Except he'd been in the field enough years to know exactly how many things could go wrong between now and happily ever after. He'd had two long years to contemplate those things. He wanted nothing more than to head for the nearest armed fortress of government agents. But he had faith that if he tried to reach any kind of government installation in this part of the country, they'd find their way blocked by a wall of AbaCo guns. He and his family just had to be patient a little while longer and let events take their course. The stakes were far too high for him to screw up the end game now.

His family…he kinda liked the sound of that.

Michelle was adorable. Of course, he hadn't had to walk the floors with her all night over colic or whatever babies got that kept them up. And she hadn't had a screaming meltdown or a stinky diaper or a food-throwing tantrum yet.

He tried to imagine the little bug doing something messy and babyish but was completely unable to muster up any real dismay at the prospect. Clearly, he was already head over heels for her.

Their destination would take them back toward Washington, D.C., but was still deep in the heart of Virginia horse country. The hour-long drive passed quickly as he studied his rearview mirror and tried to form a speech that would honestly spell out the danger they posed to their hostess without scaring off the woman entirely.

All too soon, they arrived at a mailbox that bore the number they were looking for. But beyond that, he saw nothing but a dirt path winding away into a forest. Well, he'd wanted isolated. Looked as though he'd gotten it. He turned onto the driveway.

And drove. And drove. The thing wound into what must have been a mile of woods before the trees finally gave way to rolling horse pastures and four-board oak fences on either side of the drive. They topped a hill and a towering, wrought-iron security gate blocked their way. Wow. Talk about a fortress.

Jagger pulled up before the security camera and intercom box.

Doris leaned forward. "Tell her Graminator is here."

"Graminator?" he asked gravely as Emily rolled her eyes beside him.

Doris glared. She looked prepared to turn him over her knee and spank him if he said anything more. Thankfully, a pleasant female voice came out of the intercom before he could give in to the temptation.

"Come on up to the house. Drive around back, and I'll open one of the garage doors for you. Pull in there."

He thought he detected a note of businesslike competence in the woman's voice. This might just work out after all.

The big gates swung open and he guided the car through, waiting until the gates had closed behind him to continue. No sense waxing sloppy at this late date. He eased forward and the drive topped yet another hill. He whistled through his teeth. A magnificent Colonial mansion rose out of the valley before them. Trees bordered the structure on three sides, but from this angle, a long, manicured lawn stretched from their feet all the way to the front doors.

The driveway took them down the lawn, around a four-tiered fountain and past the east end of the gracious home. As promised, when he pulled around back, one of five garage doors was invitingly open. He pulled inside, and the garage door slid shut behind them. He directed Emily and her mother to stay in the car until the door was entirely shut. And even then, he murmured for them to stay put while he checked things out.

He eased out of the car, crouching beside it, weapon drawn. He made a cautious circuit around their vehicle, ending up back at the driver's-side door.

A spill of yellow light fell into the dimly lit garage and a slender figure was silhouetted in the doorway. The same calm, businesslike voice from before said easily, "I'm unarmed but feel free to verify that for yourself."

A woman stepped forward, her hands held wide away from her body, palms up, as if she'd been checked for weapons before. She approached to within a dozen feet of him and then turned her back on him, waiting expectantly.

"I'm sorry about this," he murmured. "But I can't be too careful."

The woman answered casually, "I fully understand. I'd be equally cautious were I in your position."

He duly frisked her, keeping the exercise as quick and impersonal as possible. Then he nodded over his shoulder at the car. Emily stepped out, carrying a sleeping Michelle, followed by Doris.

Their hostess smiled. "I'm Laura Delaney. Welcome to my home. I'll do everything I can to ensure your comfort and safety during your stay here."

Jagger frowned. She sounded as though she

knew exactly what she was getting into, here. How was that? Who was this woman?

"I assume you scanned your car for tracking devices?" she asked him.

He nodded. "I found one and passed it off to a kid headed to Richmond for college."

"You only found the one?" the woman challenged.

He frowned. "I was in a rest stop. I couldn't exactly dismantle the car in the parking lot."

Quick alarm lit the woman's features. "Let me take the ladies inside and get them settled. Then I'll come back out and help you go over the car with a fine-tooth comb."

Jagger frowned. "You think there's a second device?"

"It's what I'd do if I were tracking someone I really didn't want to lose."

Crud. He really had gone soft in that box. Maybe he'd lost the edge. And now his entire family's lives were depending on him. A sharp jolt of alarm zinged him. Was he up to this fight, after all?

As they scoured the rental car for bugs,

Jagger went over the general story of his past two years. Laura offered to look into the charges against him, and it wasn't as though he was about to say no. If his boss failed to cut a deal with the FBI, he'd need to find another way to approach the bureau to arrange their surrender.

He found the second device inside the dashboard. Thankfully, it was a passive homing device and not an active transmitter that could send detailed information to AbaCo's thugs.

Jagger took great pleasure in stomping the tracker into dust. Then he asked his hostess tersely, "Do you think we should leave your place?"

"They probably know the general area in which to search for you, but I doubt they had time to triangulate your exact location. It's late and your girls are exhausted. Let's get all of you a good night's sleep and we'll figure out what to do in the morning."

The stress of the past two days was catching up with him all of a sudden. Coffee could keep him going for only so long, and the moment she mentioned sleep, a wall of fatigue slammed into him head-on. Nonetheless, he murmured gamely, "I'll stay up and watch your place."

Laura laughed. "You'll do no such thing. You're dead on your feet. I've got the watch tonight."

"You have some experience in such things?" he asked cautiously. She sounded like some sort of soldier or covert operative. She might not want to reveal her government connections, though.

She replied with equal caution, "Yes, you could say that. Suffice it to say that you should feel free to sleep very soundly. You've got nothing to worry about."

He caught the significant undertone in her voice. Yup, she was a pro. An operative of some kind. Hallelujah. They could use a little support from the home team right about now.

As Laura led the way through an enormous kitchen, she opened a broom closet and took out a lethal-looking Dragunov sniper rig. Furthermore, she looked entirely at ease handling the weapon. Holy crap. Was she more of a pro than he'd guessed? More than a government agent? Some sort of mercenary, maybe?

"Do I want to know who you are?" Jagger asked even more cautiously.

"Let's just say you and I play for the same team. Or at least we both used to."

He nodded. Fair enough. In his line of work, that was more information than many operatives would volunteer. It—and that Dragunov—were all the identification he needed. No civilian would ever have gotten her hands on the specialized military weapon. She was an operator just like him. Or maybe not just like him, but close enough.

She showed him upstairs to a two-bedroom suite joined by a sitting room. Doris was already snoring gently in one room, and Emily was curled up, unconscious, with Michelle in the king-size bed in the other room.

"Get some sleep, Mr. Holtz. And rest assured, this estate has a few security tricks up its sleeve. No one's getting near the house tonight without me knowing about it. My son and I like our privacy."

He nodded and stretched out on the sofa in the sitting room, his pistol clutched in his hand.

Which maybe didn't turn out to be such a great idea. He awoke with a jolt to bright sunlight and someone plucking his gun from his limp grasp.

"Whoa there, kiddo," he exclaimed. "That's not a toy for you, Michelle." He managed to retrieve his gun from the toddler's chubby hands just as Emily came around the corner on the hunt for the escapee.

"There you are, munch—oh. I'm sorry. I was hoping you could get a little more sleep."

He grinned up at Emily. "Not with this little kleptomaniac on the loose."

He glanced at his watch, stunned to see that it was after 9:00 a.m. He actually felt pretty close to human.

Emily announced, "I think I smell breakfast cooking. My mom got up a while ago and said she was going to go down and whip up a little something for all of us."

The mention of food sent his stomach growling against his spine. "You go on down. I'll join you in a minute."

And that was why he was alone in the upstairs hallway when Laura announced sharply from someplace toward the front of the house, "Incoming!"

Chapter 13

Emily froze at the foot of the sweeping stair-case as Jagger came barreling down from behind her, bellowing, "Get away from the windows!"

She wasn't anywhere near a window, but his shout sent her tearing toward the kitchen instinctively. He was right on her heels. Doris had already snatched up Michelle and was holding the now-crying toddler close. Jagger threw open the oven door where a batch of muffins was browning, then pulled Emily, Doris and Michelle into a giant bear hug in front of it. Heat poured out on all of them until it felt as if she were a muffin baking in the oven.

"Why are we standing in front of the oven?" Emily ventured to ask.

"We're hiding," Jagger bit out.

"Standing in plain sight?"

"We're hiding from infrared cameras."

"What?"

"Helicopter's buzzing the place," he replied tersely. "Probably scanning the house for heat signatures. The heat from the oven should obscure us from their sensors."

Comprehension lit Emily's features, followed closely by panic. "They're looking through the walls?" Her entire body vibrated in his arms as a nearly unstoppable urge to bolt tore through her.

"Just stay put, honey. All they should see in the kitchen right now is a big blob of white where the oven ought to be. Trust me," he soothed.

For Michelle's sake, she corralled her rampaging terror. But bad guys could look right into a house without so much as a by-your-leave? The thought creeped her out completely.

Their hostess, Laura, came rushing into the

kitchen. She smiled approvingly when she saw them clustered in front of the oven. "Helicopter's drawing away from the house. I wasn't sure if that meant they didn't see what they were looking for or if it meant they're going to fetch their ground forces. But after your quick thinking, Jagger, I'd say we can safely assume it is the former."

"So we're safe?" Emily asked.

"For now. They may be back, but I'll make a few phone calls. The regional air traffic control facility ought to be amenable to giving us a heads-up if any more unscheduled aircraft try to buzz this place."

Emily stared. "They'll do that for people?"

Jagger chuckled. "Not for all people, honey. But for our erstwhile hostess, I should think they would."

Emily's eyebrows shot up. Wow. Who *was* Laura Delaney? Just then a beautiful little boy with dark hair and his mother's bright blue eyes fringed in magnificent black eyelashes came running into the room. "Mommy! What's wrong? Is it the bad men again?"

Laura scooped up the child, whom Emily estimated to be around five years old. "Nope. No bad men here, Adam."

Jagger piped up. "Did you know that this lady here is called Danger Girl? She's great at keeping people she likes safe. Sometimes she even rescues them, too."

The little boy stared at her, his mouth a round O.

"Jagger," Emily muttered in disgust. "Did you have to?"

Laura started. "Danger Girl? You?"

Emily rolled her eyes. "It's an old—and bad—joke between Jagger and me. If anyone around here is superhero material, it's him and not me."

"Hmm." Laura eyed the two of them speculatively, but said no more. Emily got the feeling she'd missed something in the exchange.

The disrupted preparations for breakfast resumed. A few minutes later, a middle-aged Englishwoman whom Laura introduced as her son's nanny strolled into the general chaos. She took efficient charge of both Adam and Michelle, who were fascinated by each other, and led them off to the nether regions of the mansion to play.

As Doris's world-famous omelets slid neatly onto plates and the adults sat down at the table, Laura filled them in. Emily listened eagerly.

"Jagger, last night I took the liberty of looking into the charges against you. The evidence to support a claim of treason was turned over to the U.S. government almost two years ago. The assumption within the government has been that AbaCo made you an offer you couldn't refuse and that you'd been turned."

Emily gasped. "Jagger would never betray his country! He's the most honorable and noble man I know!"

Jagger grinned. "Thanks for the vote of confidence, but we'll need more than that to convince the feds to drop the charges against me."

"What about the fact that they had you locked up in a box for two years?" she demanded indignantly.

He sighed. "I have no proof of that."

"I let you out of that box! I'll testify to what I saw."

He sighed. "That only proves I was being held in a box two weeks ago. Nothing more."

"I saw how pale and thin you were—"

Laura cleared her throat politely. "Actually, there might be some evidence to support Jagger's claim. I can't go into the details of how I know, but I believe that AbaCo has engaged in a systematic campaign of holding prisoners on ships in international waters, in the same manner they held Jagger. I believe they kidnap some of their own hostages, but they also appear to be willing to hold other peoples' hostages for a hefty fee."

Emily wasn't sure she followed, but Jagger leaned forward intently. "You mean they're throwing people in containers like mine and just sailing around in the middle of the ocean with them indefinitely?"

Emily's stomach turned over. "You mean like a floating prison ship?"

Laura nodded grimly. "As long as the ship stays in international waters, there's not much anyone can do to help these prisoners. Only when they come into ports for refueling can anyone move on rescuing them."

Emily nodded. The *Zhow Min* had been at the Rock for just such a fuel stop when she'd freed Jagger. "Do you think more than one ship is involved? Or can we just alert the authorities to search the *Zhow Min* the next time it comes into port?"

Laura frowned. "If there is more than one ship, then the authorities will have to move very carefully. A bold rescue of the hostages on one ship might get all the others on the rest of the ships killed. Nobody knows for sure. The U.S. government dares not take any forceful action until it has proof one way or the other."

Emily chewed thoughtfully for a minute. "What about the ship's cargo manifests? Do they reflect the existence of these prisoner containers?"

Laura shrugged. "We've never managed to gain access to AbaCo's record-keeping system, but I highly doubt they'd leave an easy trail for anyone to follow."

Emily had to agree. She'd worked in the special cargo department for years, and she'd never run across any indication that such activity was taking place.

"As for the FBI charges against you, Emily," Laura commented, recapturing her attention sharply, "they're based on evidence that was turned over to the U.S. Customs Service about a week ago."

Emily winced. "I'm guilty of the things they're accusing me of. It's how I found and rescued Jagger."

Laura shrugged. "I'm certain that a competent attorney will be able to get the charges against you dropped, given the extenuating circumstances of needing to save a human life."

"I didn't technically know I was saving a human life. I was given a hint to peek into a certain container, and when I did, I stumbled across Jagger."

Laura smiled serenely. "It's all about how a good attorney spins it. I think you'll be all right. As for you, Jagger, it would be helpful if we could prove that AbaCo's holding prisoners in international waters. Your claims would be that much more believable."

He sighed. "They're careful. And my departure from their floating accommodations was rather abrupt. It's not like I stuck around to gather evidence to prove that I was their prisoner for two years."

"Understood. We'll just have to catch them doing something else dastardly and take pictures next time."

Jagger snorted and Emily echoed the sentiment. She'd worked for AbaCo long enough to know just how smart and devious her ex-employer could be. The next time the company slipped up could be a long time in coming.

Laura turned to her abruptly. "Emily, have you checked to see if your AbaCo computer passwords have been revoked?"

"I'm sure they were the moment I was discovered missing."

"Too bad. It would've been exceedingly helpful in helping clear Jagger's name to have been able to get into their system."

Emily grinned. "I didn't say I couldn't get

into their system. I merely said my passwords were revoked."

Laura leaned forward. "Do tell."

"I happen to know my boss's passwords and those of about half my coworkers."

Jagger and Laura exchanged pregnant glances. He muttered, "They could use the break-in to track where you live."

"And they could run into the blind firewall my server throws up against traces," Laura retorted confidently.

Jagger shrugged. "Your call. I'm all over any help you can give us, but you're in no way obligated to endanger yourself or your son."

"Actually, I am obligated. It's what I do."

"Come again?"

Emily was glad Jagger asked the question. She was definitely lost now.

"I help people. Particularly moms. Single moms. It's how I pass the time. I'd go crazy rattling around this big house by myself without having projects to work on. Apparently, you folks are my latest project."

Emily liked the sound of that. Their hostess

seemed remarkably connected to influential people and seemed to have no shortage of other resources to draw on.

After breakfast, Laura and Jagger disappeared into a sumptuous library on the ground floor to map out a strategy of what they were going to do when they broke into AbaCo's computers. Once they had it all worked out, then they would call her in to sign on to the company's database.

She spent most of the morning playing with Adam and Michelle. The little boy was bright and charming, much like his mother. There was one brief scare when what turned out to be a deer tripped some sort of motion detector on the grounds of the estate. She didn't think she'd ever get used to seeing Jagger whip out a gun and race around like some sort of trained killer.

Although to hear him and Laura talking casually about defense plans for the mansion, it sounded as though that was what both of them were. A few weeks ago, that concept would have scared her silly. But now…now she was thrilled that he was every bit as violently trained as he was. It was a relief to have him on her and Michelle's side.

It was nearly lunchtime when Jagger called her into the office. "Okay, darlin'. If you can get us into the cargo database, we'll take it from there."

She sat down in front of the state-of-the-art computer system and its twin plasma screens. "Do you want into the regular cargo tracking system or the special one?"

Jagger and Laura stared at her. He spoke first. "You can still get us into the special one?"

"Sure."

A slow grin spread across his face. "By all means, then. Hack away."

She typed rapidly, bringing up the hidden sign-on screen. Dieter Uling, the guy who did her job on the Rock when she was rotated off the island, never changed his passwords, and he hadn't in the past week, either, it turned out. She signed on in his name and then stood up. "Have fun, you two."

Jagger was already seated at the desk, typing

rapidly. A scrolling list of outstanding shipments rolled down the screen. "Do you know
how to get this to print?"

Emily snorted. "Of course. Move over." She
leaned over him, typed in a set of commands
and the printer beside her began to hum.

"Is there any way to tell what's in each of
these shipments?" Laura asked.

Emily shook her head regretfully. "No. The
actual contents of these special containers are
only kept in hard copy. The ship's captain gets
a set, and the customer retains a set. We destroy all other records as soon as the cargo's
delivered."

"Which, in and of itself, is pretty incriminating," Jagger murmured.

"We maintain a list of the weight of each
shipment, and in some cases, we record a haz-
ardous materials status."

"But for the most part, you could be moving
absolutely anything in those boxes and nobody
would know."

Emily nodded. "I can show you how AbaCo
runs phantom weight and balance measure-

ments for the ships to account for the invisible containers. Here's one, right now, in fact." She pointed at the screen and a complicated set of entries beside a cargo shipment. "This is a normal shipment, but it's been linked to a phantom container. This set of numbers is the load plan corrections for the second container."

Jagger muttered, "This is a gold mine."

Laura added, "Print all you can now. We may have to back out of the system fast once they realize we're not signed on from an AbaCo office."

Emily hit the Print All command, and she'd no sooner hit the enter key than the second computer screen lit up with all kinds of security warnings.

Laura announced, "That's our cue, folks. Shut 'er down."

Jagger hit the escape button and the screen went blank.

The computer continued to spit out paper for several minutes; however, the data had successfully been batched over to the printer's internal memory before AbaCo spotted the break-in and cut off the database.

Jagger eagerly removed a thick sheaf of papers from the printer. "Let's take a look at this stuff and see if we can spot anything to take to the feds and clear our names."

Emily said, "What can I do to help? There must be something. I want to stop these guys once and for all."

Jagger snorted. "You and me both." Then he suggested, "Perhaps you could translate some of these numbers into plain English for us."

She spent several minutes going over the entries with him and Laura, explaining what the abbreviations meant until the pair had the hang of reading the information.

Jagger reached across the table to squeeze her hand gratefully. His touch was casual, intimate. As if he was perfectly at ease with claiming her as his in front of someone else.

Her face heated up as he murmured, "I think with this information, you may have just saved our future together. It looks at a first pass through this stuff like we'll be able to nail AbaCo with it."

Emily stared. To heck with AbaCo. He was talking about "their future together"? Was Jagger seriously contemplating sticking around, then? She'd hoped…but she'd dared not believe. Her heart leaped in her chest at the thought of him in her and Michelle's life for the long term. Of holidays and birthday parties and first dates experienced as a family. But she still couldn't let herself think the word *forever*. Even Danger Girl knew better than to reach that high with her dreams.

A need to be alone, to process the idea of Jagger as a fully involved father, overcame her. She murmured an excuse and rose to leave. "If you guys need anything from me, just give a shout."

He grinned. "You've already been more help than you can imagine."

Emily wandered in several times over the next few hours and answered various questions about notations and company procedures as Jagger and Laura sorted through the documents. She wished there were more she could do. Jagger assured her that most intelligence work was like this—a few moments of terror punctuated by hours and hours of tedium, or worse, sifting through piles of boring data.

Laura had sent the nanny out for the weekend with a flimsy excuse about the woman working far too hard. But Emily suspected it had more to do with not exposing her to possible danger. Besides, Doris was having a ball with the kids and had them well in hand.

Emily and her mother fed the kids lunch and carried plates in to Jagger and Laura a little after noon. That was when Laura suggested casually that if Emily would like to check her e-mail she should feel free to jump online. It dawned on Emily belatedly that it had been a while since she'd checked her messages. In fact, the last e-mail she'd received had been that cryptic message that led her to Jagger.

She sat down at the computer cautiously. "And you guys are sure AbaCo isn't tracking my e-mail and won't find me if I sign on?"

Jagger laughed. "Not on this system, they

won't find you. It's locked up tighter than Fort Knox."

Laura added laughingly, "Actually, the system will route AbaCo to an address in a slum in Mumbai. I'd love to see their guys running around there in hundred-degree heat and humidity trying to track you down. You can't believe the stench of the place in the summer."

Grinning at the notion, Emily signed online. She deleted a pile of junk mail, and then spied an e-mail address that made her pulse pound. MysteryMom. The source of that cryptic message had sent her another post. And the time-date group on it was barely an hour old.

In trepidation, she opened the message.

Veronique. 3L6H2D.

"What's wrong, Em?" Jagger asked immediately.

"I got another message. Just like the one that led me to you."

"What does it say?"

She read the message aloud.

"What does it mean?" Jagger asked.

"The *Veronique* is one of AbaCo's ships. And I assume the numbers and letters are another set of coordinates that will lead to a specific container."

"Can you access information on the *Veronique* online?" Laura asked innocently.

Emily shrugged. "I suppose so. I'd better use someone else's security code, though. I imagine ol' Dieter's having a pretty bad day right about now."

She signed in to the general AbaCo database, this time using the code of a fellow clerk from her stint in Denver.

"The *Veronique* is due in to Norfolk tomorrow night. The container at that cargo position is another reefer unit like the one I found you in, Jagger."

"Reefer?"

"Refrigerated unit. It has a self-contained generator that holds its contents at a constant temperature."

Jagger swore under his breath. "Do you suppose they've got another poor schmuck stashed in the back of the thing?"

Emily stared at him. "You think Mystery-Mom has found out where they're holding another prisoner and wants us to find him or her?"

He shrugged. "It makes sense. The whole reason I was sent in to infiltrate AbaCo in the first place was that we'd lost two operatives to them in under a year. They just disappeared. No trace. Just…gone."

Emily added grimly, "And you made three. How many more since then has Uncle Sam lost?"

Jagger shrugged. "Hopefully, they quit trying with me. I'd hate to think someone came in to rescue me and got captured, too."

Into the heavy silence that followed, Laura commented quietly, "If we were able to recover another prisoner and document the conditions of his captivity, it would go a long way toward corroborating your story. This time, pictures should be taken, maybe some video shot, during the rescue."

"AbaCo's got to be edgy after my escape. I highly doubt we'd be able to stroll aboard and just turn the guy loose like Emily did with me."

Laura shrugged. "So, we'll prepare more carefully, knowing that we have to plan for opposition to our extraction. No biggie."

Emily exclaimed, "Are you two nuts? AbaCo's trying to kill us and the FBI's trying to catch us, and you want to just waltz onto a giant ship in the middle of a busy port, which by the way will be crawling with government officials, and break into a container?"

Jagger commented tightly, "AbaCo's a big company. They can't watch everywhere at once. And of course we'll set up a diversion."

"Of course," Emily repeated drily.

The strain in his voice was palpable as he ground out, "Honey, if there's even the slightest chance that some other guy is stuck in a box wasting away and not another living soul knows he's there, I *have* to do something about it."

"But you have no idea if there's even anyone in this container," she protested.

"We'll figure out a way to tell. Can you look at the corrected weight on the load plan and see if this container actually weighs what it's supposed to for a load of—" he glanced down at the papers in front of him on the desk "—live orchid plants?"

Emily frowned. "I suppose I could check it out." She moved over to the desk. "Plants are a low-density cargo, but orchids need a humidifier system in the container, which adds a couple hundred pounds of motors and water." She pulled out a pen and paper. "What does the open manifest say the weight of that reefer is?"

Jagger rattled the number off and she jotted it down.

Then she asked, "Laura, can you find a load correction to any of the containers immediately surrounding that box?"

It took a minute, but the other woman exclaimed in satisfaction, "Here it is. Negative eighty-two hundred pounds and negative rolling moment of .023 degrees."

Emily ran through the calculations. Her stomach sank at the end result. Reluctantly, she announced, "That weight reduction would account for approximately one-third of the plants in the container. Which means the odds are excellent that there's a relatively large open area in that reefer, similar in volume to the one you were held in, Jagger. Or else they're smuggling air."

Jagger's jaw rippled grimly. "I can't turn my back on this lead. I've got to rescue whoever's in that box."

Emily's gut clenched in denial. She'd just found him! She couldn't risk losing him again so soon. And not this way. Not shot up or worse by the very people who'd captured him and torn the two of them apart in the first place. Both of them had already lost far too much to AbaCo. "*Please,* Jagger, call the police."

"We need the evidence, Em. We've got to move in fast and get it before AbaCo can pay anyone off to tamper with or destroy the evidence. By the time we call the police, present our evidence, they decide to move, then they get both the local and federal warrants they'll need to search the ship, the *Veronique* will be long gone. AbaCo will send it back out into international waters where no one can touch it. If the guy in that container is lucky, all they'll do is push his box overboard. If not, they'll torture him to try to figure out who's coming after him."

"But a rescue now, especially after you escaped, will be terribly dangerous—"

He cut her off. "I'm fully aware of that. Which is why I'll be careful."

"Why *we'll* be careful," Laura amended firmly.

Panic squeezed Emily's throat until she couldn't force out the words to tell Jagger how much she feared losing him. How he couldn't do this to her and Michelle. How he had to give up this foolishness—give up his career, if need be—rather than put himself at this kind of risk. She and their daughter needed him. Instead, all that came out of her mouth was a muted sound of protest.

Laura spoke gently, "Emily, it really is a golden opportunity to clear your names and catch AbaCo red-handed all in one fell swoop."

Laura was right. Emily's rational brain could accept the truth of that, but her gut was another matter entirely. Despairing, she looked over at Jagger. He came around the table to her, lifted her to her feet and wrapped her in the comforting safety of his embrace.

He murmured, "I promise it'll be okay. I know what I'm doing, honey. It'll turn out fine."

She closed her eyes and buried her face against his chest. She wished she could be half so confident. No way could she let him walk out the door by himself, leaving her to wait and wonder. That would kill her for sure.

He went on, "But I *have* to do this. I couldn't live with myself if I didn't do it."

She loosed a shuddering sigh that was half a sob. He was right. And after all, she'd heard his delirious rantings. She knew better than anyone how much he needed to take action after two years of helplessness, to get retribution against AbaCo in some way. She was going to lose this fight. Heck, she'd already lost it.

She reached for courage she wasn't even

sure she had and raised her head. She wiped the tears from her cheeks and announced as bravely as Danger Girl could, "If you're absolutely set on going through with this, then you two are going to need my help."

Jagger smiled down at her in relief and gratitude. "Thank you, Emily. I know this is hard for you. And for the record, I'm counting on your help."

She shook her head and crushed an urge to continue trying to talk him out of it. It was a waste of breath—she knew that stubborn set of the jaw all too well from Michelle. She muttered in resignation, "You know this is crazy, right?"

"Crazy's my middle name, darlin'." His cocky grin faded. "And besides, I owe AbaCo one. I'll bring down those bastards if it's the last thing I do."

Emily flinched. She had a sinking feeling it might very well be the last thing he ever did if he tangled with AbaCo.

Chapter 14

Jagger invited Emily to join him and Laura after supper for a closed-door planning session. She told them everything she could think of about AbaCo security procedures and cargo-handling routines. But when they got down to the nitty-gritty of practicing how to work together in a gunfight, she visibly panicked. Her hands began to shake and her breath trembled, and she couldn't seem to sit still in her seat.

He took pity. "The rest of this planning is just technical stuff, Em. Besides, isn't it getting close to Michelle's bedtime? I bet she'd love to have her mommy tuck her in."

Emily snorted. "I dunno. Granny's a push-over when it comes to Michelle wheedling more time to play out of her. I'm the bedtime Nazi."

Jagger grinned. It was hard to imagine sweet Emily being a Nazi about anything.

Her calm facade evaporated as she rose to her feet and excused herself. Poor kid. She was running a lot closer to the edge of falling apart than she'd been letting on. He had to give her credit, though. She was stronger than she looked. She'd been a champ so far. Just one more day and this mess would be resolved, assuming everything went well.

And if things went bad, well, then not much would matter at all.

He and Laura compared notes and figured out quickly that their respective training had come pretty much out of the same playbook. Which was a huge relief.

Laura excused herself to go tuck in Adam, and he wandered upstairs, gravitating toward the squeals of laughter emanating from Michelle and Doris's bathroom. The door was partially open and he peeked in.

His daughter was sitting up to her chin in a

mountain of bubbles, and had them piled on her head and hanging from her chin in a fair toddler imitation of Santa Claus. Emily and Doris were laughing, and the scene was so endearing he felt something in his heart break at the sight.

All of it could be his. The laughter, the love, the sense of family. All he had to do was reach out and take it.

Tomorrow. He just had to get through tomorrow. And then he'd take everything they had to offer him and more. He'd reach for it all.

Michelle's hands emerged from the mounds of bubbles and slapped down on the water, sending bubbles flying every which way, and drenching Emily and Doris. Michelle squealed with renewed laughter, delighted at the liberal glops of bubbles now adorning the two women.

He didn't think he'd ever get enough of that sweet sound. His daughter's laughter was a balm to his soul. As he stood there in the shadows of the doorway and watched the hilarity, the crack in his heart split wider and wider until the whole thing burst apart in an explosion of joy.

He was *happy.*

Happier than he could ever remember being. And it was all because of the laughter of a child. His child. *Their* child. The daughter he and Emily had created and whom she had shared with him in an act of generosity that stole his breath away.

Emily plucked the toddler from the water and wrapped her in a towel that swallowed Michelle whole. He retreated while Emily dried the child and dressed her in a fuzzy pair of pink footed jammies that were too cute to be legal. No doubt about it, his daughter would have daddy wrapped around her little finger in no time flat. The truth of the matter was he was already a goner.

He lurked in the next room while Emily rocked Michelle to sleep, closing his eyes and letting the quiet lullaby she sang wash over him like a blessing. And he'd thought he loved Emily before. Seeing her like this, loving his child with the full measure of a mother's devotion, filled up spaces in this new heart of his that he'd never dreamed existed.

When Emily moved to get up a while later, he glided into the room quickly and lifted Michelle from her arms. Together, they carried their daughter to the crib Laura had thoughtfully provided and tucked their angel in snugly for the night.

Jagger looped his arm over Emily's shoulder as they turned to leave.

He stopped just inside their bedroom. "She's awesome, Em. You've done an amazing job with her."

Emily blushed a little. "I'm sure I've made my share of mistakes, but I figure if you just love them with everything you've got, the rest will take care of itself."

He'd give anything if she could love him that much. But they'd thought a lot of hurtful things about each other over the past two years. He didn't know how long it would take for her to trust him completely again. Thankfully, Aba-Co's lies about her had been exposed, and he'd let go of his need to hurt her. He shuddered to think, though, of what might have happened if she had not been the one to rescue him. Would he have ever believed in her innocence otherwise? Would he have thrown away bubble baths and fuzzy jammies and soothing lullabies in the name of vengeance? He feared he would have. And the thought left him chilled to the bone.

"Hey, are you okay?" Emily asked in concern. "You look pale."

He grinned bravely. "I'm fine. It's just the lighting. Super Spies don't get pale."

Emily grinned back. "Well, Danger Girl certainly does. She gets scared to death and isn't afraid to admit it."

He swept her into his arms and grinned down at her as her eyes went limpid. "Right now, Danger Girl looks a little flushed."

She murmured up at him, "You do that to me."

"I know. And I love it. Come." He drew her toward the big bed that was invitingly turned down. "Let's see how much of you is blushing for me."

Emily laughed. "That would be all of me, you forward man."

He expected to make love to Emily, but she surprised him by pushing him down gently to the mattress and indicating that he should roll onto his stomach. She checked his wounds, which were healing nicely, and then she gave him the mother of all back rubs. He was putty in her hands. But when she rolled him over onto his back and gave his front the same loving attention, tension built in him until he couldn't stand it any longer.

He rolled over, taking her with him, and stared deep into her eyes as their bodies became one. The intimacy of the moment was almost more than he could stand. But generous Emily never flinched, never pulled back. She opened her body and heart to him and gave him every last bit of herself without reservation. It was almost as if she was offering him the very sense of family and belonging he'd craved earlier.

When the shudders of their lovemaking finally died away, she reached up, smiling lazily, to cup the back of his neck with her hand. She murmured, "I could do that for the rest of my life and never get tired of it."

"Is that an invitation to stick around awhile?" he replied.

She stared up at him intently. "Yes. It is. You know I'd love to be with you for as long as you'll have me."

For as long as he'd have her? His mind spun out the possibilities of that. "I think, honey, that could be a very long time, indeed."

She smiled, but the expression didn't penetrate the darkness in her eyes. "Then how can you stand to risk all of this—you and me, being there for Michelle, our *family?*"

With her body still warm around his, the love in her eyes reaching out to embrace him, their daughter sleeping in the next room, he could see her point. Did he really dare chance losing all of this? For a possible prisoner, a stranger he'd never met and wasn't even sure existed?

Doubt sliced into him, sharp and hot. She had a point. Maybe his days as a superspy were over. Maybe he was clinging to a part of himself that no longer existed. What if he'd lost the edge? The possible consequences of failure were too awful to contemplate. So why was he trying it?

Emily stared up at him, no doubt watching the arguments play out in his eyes. She murmured, "I knew I could make you change your mind. I just had to get you away from Laura and remind you about your family—"

Abruptly angry, he cut her off. "So this sweet seduction was just a case of bedroom politics? You were just trying to get me to change my mind?"

She frowned. "No, well, yes. Yes, I was hoping you'd change your mind. But no, it wasn't just about that. I lo—"

He rolled away from her and out of the bed, striding across the room to pick up his discarded clothes. He yanked them on angrily. "I'm not that gullible. I know what I have to do and nothing you say or do is going to change that, dammit!"

To her credit, she didn't try to argue with him.

He stormed out of the room and headed downstairs.

It took him all of about five minutes to calm down and realize he'd overreacted. She was only looking out for Michelle. She wanted her daughter to have a father. He couldn't fault the impulse. And besides, he'd give almost anything to be able to settle down and raise Michelle with her. But unfortunately, he was still Super Spy, and he still had responsibilities.

First on that list was clearing their names so she could have the peaceful life she craved with her daughter. Second, and no less important, was evening the score with AbaCo so he could live in peace with the events of the past two years. Those were more important than any fairy-tale, happily-ever-after scenario she envisioned.

He pulled out the schematics of the *Veronique* that Laura had found online and printed earlier and he pored over them, walking through the plan a dozen times in his head, trying to anticipate absolutely every possible scenario for tomorrow night's rescue. It—he—must not fail.

A long time later, he crawled into bed beside Emily and gathered her warmth against his side.

She murmured sleepily, "Did you finish planning World War Three?"

"As much as I can. Operations like this never go according to plan. A certain amount of improvisation is inevitable."

He felt Emily's wince against his shoulder. She mumbled, "That's the part that worries me. All that unpredictable stuff that can go wrong."

"Don't worry too much about it. Sometimes things break the good guy's way, too. It all evens out in the end."

"Yeah, well, I found you and freed you, and that's about as much as I'm willing to demand from fate."

He smiled into the darkness. "Sleep, honey. One more day and it'll all be over."

He thought he heard her mumble under her breath, "And then what?"

He didn't have an answer for her. Not yet. He had to focus entirely on the moment at hand and not to lose concentration by speculating about a future he couldn't guarantee that they'd have. He could only pray that the Fates had one more lucky break lined up to fall his way.

He slept deeply. So deeply that when he lurched upright, sweating and sure he was back in that damned box, he didn't know where he was right away. He threw off the covers, which felt far too much like ropes tying him down. His old scars ached and he rubbed them to convince the nerves there that they were not under attack.

The dark of the bedroom was as oppressive as the blackness of his crate and played tricks on his mind until he slipped out of bed and padded over to the door to Michelle's room. He cracked it open to admit the glow of her nightlight.

He couldn't resist. He tiptoed into her room to peer down at the little girl. She slept on her stomach, sprawled in abandon, with one arm flung over a rather tattered plush bunny. Her blond curls tangled around her face, and her one visible cheek was chubby and rosy. Calmed by the sight of her, he padded back to bed and left the adjoining door open a bit.

No doubt about it. If another man was caged up in a box, missing these perfect moments with his family, Jagger had to take action. He *had* to try to save the guy.

Chapter 15

Emily crouched behind Jagger and Laura and wondered yet again how Jagger did this for a living. The sneaking around guards and over fences they'd had to do to even get to this dock had wiped her out physically and emotionally, and they hadn't even started the real mission yet.

Jagger murmured, "Is that the *Veronique?*"

She whispered back, "That's the right slip, and she's about the right size. I can't see her name from here, though."

Laura pointed to a stack of truck-sized containers not far from the pier to which the *Veronique* was tied. "I'm heading over there.

I'll radio you to confirm that we've got the right ship. Then you can do your thing, Emily."

Right. Her thing. Boldly walking aboard the ship with her expired AbaCo identification and hoping against hope she didn't trigger any alarms that got her detained or worse. Jagger swore they'd rescue her if that happened, but Danger Girl was a quivering puddle of terror at the moment.

Laura darted across an open space and disappeared into the shadows beside the containers. Her radio call was all too quick in coming. "Yup, it's our ship. You're on, Emily."

Jagger stood up in front of her and she did the same. She gazed up at him in wordless fear, and without her having to ask, he wrapped her in his warm, safe arms. "It'll be all right, honey. Just stick to the plan. We'll be right behind you."

Right. Stick to the plan. She could do this. *Not.* What if it was all a giant trap?

Jagger must have sensed the direction her thoughts were taking because he murmured,

"We can handle whatever happens. I know you can do this. Do it for me."

Darn it. Did he have to go and say the one thing that would prevent her from turning tail and running as fast as her feet would go? She nodded reluctantly against his chest. "Have you got the video camera?"

"Yup, everything's ready. It's time, honey."

He released her and took a step back. One gloved finger traced down her cheek and along the line of her jaw. "Be careful. If it looks like you're not going to make it, back out. Don't be a hero—we'll find another way to get aboard."

Right. No heroes here.

She took a deep breath, turned away from him and took a step. And then another. Before she knew it, her feet had carried her into the peach glow of the halogen lights bathing the pier. She walked almost halfway down the starboard side of the massive container ship and onto the aluminum gangplank leading into the bowels of the vessel.

"Can I help you?" a sailor asked in gruff surprise.

"Yes, you can. I'm with the special cargo division at AbaCo, and there's a problem with the paperwork on a shipment aboard the *Veronique*. The load plan you guys faxed to our office doesn't match the one we have on file. I'm going to have to go through the deck load container by container and figure out which setup is accurate." She rolled her eyes in disgust at the snafu.

"Oh, man, that sucks." The guy commiserated.

She fluttered her eyelashes at him, not enough to be outright flirting, but enough to capture his attention, nonetheless. Keeping eye contact with him, she pulled out her AbaCo identification badge and clipped it to her belt at her waist. Then she shifted her clipboard to partially conceal it.

"Is there any chance you could show me how to get topside? I get lost in these big ships. And—" she leaned in close to confess as the guy's pupils dilated "—I'm a little claustrophobic. Sometimes I get kinda freaked out in ships' passageways. I don't know how you do it."

On cue, the sailor puffed up. "Oh, you get used to it. You just tough it out at first, ya know."

He turned and headed down the narrow, dimly lit passage behind him. "C'mon. I'll walk you up top. Main stairwell's this way."

She refrained from glancing over her shoulder into the shadows. Somewhere very close behind her, Jagger and Laura were waiting to dart aboard the *Veronique* in the absence of the man on watch. If all went well, they'd take another stairwell and meet her on deck in a few minutes.

Her helpful sailor led her out into a towering jungle of stacked containers, looming so high overhead they cut off all but the tiniest sliver of night sky.

"Need some help?"

Emily looked around with a sigh. "Nah. I'll give a holler up to the bridge if I need any help. I've got the phone number."

"Right, then. I'd better get back to the hatch. I'll see ya when you're finished."

Emily smiled warmly. "See you in a little while."

Thankfully, he didn't stick around to flirt any longer and left her to herself. She moved farther into the containers. The one she sought would be in the aft half of the ship, near the centerline of the vessel. Jagger was concerned that it would be visible from the bridge. He and Laura had some sort of diversion planned just in case.

There it was. A rusty brown, temperature-controlled unit that wasn't the slightest bit re-markable. Was it possible that a human being was caged up in there? The container was about fifteen feet up, in the third layer of containers. This time, no rolling staircase was nearby to make access easy. She moved to the end of the row of containers and stepped close to the rail to look overboard. Oily black water swirled nearly a hundred feet below. She gulped and took a quick step back.

She leaped violently when a male voice came from the shadows directly behind her. "Hey, baby, wanna get naked with me?"

"Jagger!" she snapped under her breath. "You scared me to death."

"Work your way down this outside row of containers, and pretend to compare lading numbers to your sheets of paper. A guy on the bridge has binoculars on you."

Holy smokes. Someone was watching her? The back of her neck crawled. She hastily flipped a few pages of her fake notes and then pretended to study the packing documents pasted in a clear plastic pouch on the side of the nearest container.

Jagger murmured from the shadows again, "Laura's gonna watch the other end of the aisle while I enter the unit. Drop your clipboard and cry out like you startled yourself if you see anyone coming this way."

And then he was gone. She was alone and exposed. She moved on to the next container and repeated her paperwork charade.

She'd been at it maybe three minutes and had made her way back to near the narrow aisle between stacks of containers when she heard Jagger's voice call out low, "Em. Come here."

What on earth? That wasn't part of the plan. She strolled unconcernedly into the aisle in case the man on the bridge was still watching her. The bulk of the bridge tower disappeared from view. She sprinted to where the container door was barely cracked open.

"What's up?" she murmured as loud as she dared.

"I need your help. There's a guy in here, but he's in pretty bad shape. I'm sending him down on a rope, but he may need your help."

They'd done it! They'd found another prisoner. Now, if they could get him off the ship, they'd have all the proof they needed to sink AbaCo and clear their names!

Her pulse leaped in trepidation as the door opened wider and a shadowed form backed out of the box on his hands and knees. It turned out Jagger had rigged a loop in the rope for the prisoner to step into with his foot. Jagger lowered the man by letting the rope slide slowly down to the deck.

The man was tall with a heavy black beard, but so emaciated he looked hollow. He staggered as he stepped out of the rope and Emily wedged a shoulder under his armpit to steady him.

"Problem, Jagger," Laura called out low from somewhere out of sight nearby. "A couple of AbaCo guys are headed this way with purpose. They don't look like grunts."

"Armed?" Jagger asked quickly.

"Not visibly," was the low response. "We've got to go. Now."

Jagger slithered down the rope fast and joined Emily and the tall man. "Em, any chance you can head those AbaCo guys off while we get our friend out of sight? He's not in any condition to run. We're gonna have to hide him until the goons leave."

She blinked fast. "Uh, I'll try." Crap. She was terrible at improvising.

Laura rounded the corner and skidded to a stop in front of them. "Let's go with the zip lines over the port rail—" She broke off, staring at the prisoner. "Nick?" she whispered.

The man's head jerked up. His dull eyes grew slightly less dead. "Laura?" he croaked.

"Oh, my God," Laura cried softly. She took a step forward as if to embrace the fellow, but Jagger spoke in a sharp whisper. "Save it. We've got to go. Our friend can't handle anything strenuous like climbing ropes. We've got to hide him until we can sneak him outta here."

Laura nodded and batted at the tears streaming down her face. The man, Nick, looped his arm possessively around the woman's shoulders and the two of them shuffled slowly toward the port side of the ship.

Jagger muttered to Emily, "Keep your story simple." And then he whirled and caught up in a few strides with the couple's painfully slow progress.

Emily headed out fast to intercept the incoming AbaCo men. When she heard their footsteps about to round the corner, she stopped and commenced examining the bill of lading on the nearest container.

"Oh!" She cried out as three men came into sight and all but slammed into her. "Goodness, you startled me!"

"I'm Robert Schmeckler, ma'am. Ship's security officer. Forgive me for being blunt, but who are you? And please explain exactly what it is you're doing here."

She remembered hearing somewhere that the best defense was a good offense. A vision of Laura in tears over that starving man fresh in her mind's eye, Emily scowled and put on her best indignant tone. "I work for Hans Schroder in the Special Cargo Division. I'm *supposed* to be on vacation in Washington, D.C., right now, but he called me up from the Rock and insisted I come down here to check out an irregularity with the *Veronique's* load plan. Is one of you gentlemen responsible for it? He's going to want to speak to you tomorrow."

The three men reacted to Schroder's name and the mention of the Rock. None of them took credit, or blame as the case might be, for being in charge of the ship's load plan. Which was a relief. A true load planner would know immediately that she was blowing smoke.

She went on in tones of disgust. "Frankly, I don't know what he's talking about. Everything looks perfectly in order to me. I think the paperwork got screwed up on his end, and I'm going to tell him that as soon as I get back from my *interrupted* vacation."

"May I see your credentials?" Schmeckler asked in his deadpan German accent.

There was no help for it. She handed her ID badge over to him. He studied it closely for a minute. "This badge is expired, Miss Grainger."

She rolled her eyes. "I'm fully aware of that. I told Hans I hadn't had time to renew it before I left Hawaii, but he insisted I come down here anyway. Go ahead and throw me off the ship. It would serve him right. I swear, I'm gonna make him give me an extra week of vacation after this fiasco."

"I'll have to keep this badge."

Emily snorted. "Be my guest."

"I also have to ask you to come with me."

Ohgodohgodohgod. Michelle! If these guys arrested her, how would her daughter grow up without her?

She mumbled, "Uh, of course. Lead on." What else could she do? She couldn't possibly outrun these guys, and she'd die, literally, if she jumped overboard and splatted herself on the pier below.

The security officer turned and led the way while the other two men pointedly fell in behind her. They stepped through a hatchway and into the main superstructure of the ship. It was a short walk to a cramped office, and Schmeckler waved her to one of two chairs in front of his desk.

She jammed her hands in the pockets of her jacket and sat down where he indicated. She was *so* busted. Was she the next victim they'd throw into a container and forget? Or wouldn't she be that lucky? No way could she hold out against the kind of torture Jagger had endured. And what about Michelle? Her baby needed a mother! What on *earth* had she been thinking to go along with Jagger on this wild escapade?

She wasn't Danger Girl. She never had been. She'd always been that cautious little mouse who overdressed for bad weather in case she had car trouble. All her efforts to change—to become the kind of woman a man like Jagger

Holtz might love—had been in vain. And stupid. Extremely stupid. He'd chosen the mission over her—he hadn't changed one bit. He would breeze back out of her life as quickly as he'd breezed into it.

Except in the meantime, she'd gotten into a mess way over her head, and her daughter was going to be the one to pay. This was absurd. She just wanted to go home, live a quiet life and watch her daughter grow up in peace. To heck with all this action and adventure. Jagger could have it.

"I'll need to call Schroder and verify your identity, Miss Grainger."

She nodded stiffly, and was vaguely surprised that her neck didn't shatter with the strain of that small movement. In desperation, she blurted, "It's the wee hours of the morning on the Rock. He may not answer his phone. He's prone to turning it off at some point in the night so he can get a few hours of uninterrupted sleep. But he usually comes into the office around 8:00 a.m. Hawaii time. That's just a couple of hours from now. We can wait till then to call him if we have to."

As she spoke, she groped in her right pocket for her new cell phone. She counted number pads with her fingertips and dialed Schroder's cell phone. She covered the entire phone with her palm and pressed its face tightly against her thigh, praying it would sufficiently mute the sound of her call ringing at the other end. Not to mention, she didn't want Schroder to hear any of what was going on at this end.

Schmeckler dialed his desk phone and waited impatiently.

Please, God, let my call go through first and block the line.

The security guy frowned. "I'm getting a busy signal."

She nodded knowingly. "Ah. The lines to the Rock are either all busy or down temporarily. We have to rely on satellites, and when sun spots flare up, phone service out there gets iffy. Especially the personal phone lines. If you wait a few minutes and try again, they may come back up."

Schmeckler asked one of the men hovering behind her. "Where's Zook?"

"Ashore with your conting—"

With a sudden, alarmed glance in her direction, Schmeckler made a sharp hand gesture that cut the first man off, midsyllable.

Emily frowned. Schmeckler's contingent of what? Men? What would an AbaCo security officer send a contingent of sailors ashore to do? The way the first man said it, she didn't get the impression the sailors had been sent ashore to get drunk and pick up women. And who was Zook, anyway? Assuming that was the name of an actual person?

Schmeckler looked over at her and explained from behind a falsely saccharine smile, "He's the ship's load master."

Thank God *he* was off the ship. Yet a little more time she'd bought for her partners in crime to find a way off the vessel. Meanwhile, she had to occupy Schmeckler so he wouldn't think up some creative way around Schroder's busy cell phone.

She leaned forward. "While we're waiting, if

you'll pull up the ship's load plan, I'll show you the anomalies in the weight and balance that we're concerned about." She lowered her voice. "As you well know, the company occasionally carries cargo for clients that is best left…discreetly accounted for."

Schmeckler's eyebrows shot straight up. He obviously knew exactly what she was talking about, but seemed startled that she knew about it, too.

She shrugged. "I'm in charge of burying the money trail. Of course I know where everything—" she paused before adding significantly "—and everyone is."

Schmeckler typed on his computer and then gestured her to come around his desk.

She thought fast, and only one idea came to her. It was wildly risky, but what other choice did she have? She'd do whatever it took at this point to get out of here and get back to Michelle. *And she'd never, ever, leave her daughter's side again.*

"May I?" she asked, reaching for the keyboard.

The man at her elbow nodded.

"Take, for example, the temperature-controlled unit in this position." She scrolled down to the container from which they'd just rescued Nick. "As you know, its cargo has a significantly lower weight than live plants."

The guy beside her looked thunderstruck that she was aware of that particular container. Some of the suspicion around his eyes seemed to ease as she proved that she was an extreme insider into AbaCo's extracurricular activities.

She continued pleasantly. "The weight correction for our passenger unit should have been made to this container over here." She randomly pointed at a container that was shown as loaded on the opposite side of the *Veronique*. She said a quick mental prayer that Schmeckler wasn't any great expert at load planning and continued. "But there's no notation of a load correction. That's what Hans Schroder is freaking out over. If something were to happen to this ship, the paperwork would get examined with a fine-tooth comb and then people would starting opening up containers to have a look."

She had no idea what people would open which containers, but it seemed to scare the heck out of Schmeckler.

Just then, a walkie-talkie sitting on his desk blared, and Emily jumped about a foot in the air. A voice crackled across it, "Sir, we may have an intruder on board. We just got a hit on a motion detector on deck four, and we show no personnel in that area."

Schmeckler cursed. Her German was good enough to pick out him complaining to himself about being short-handed tonight and not needing this with one of Schroder's people sitting in front of him.

Emily moved smoothly back over to the chair in front of his desk. "I'll wait here if that's something you need to go check out. Lock me in, if you want to. That way you can take your men with you."

Schmeckler frowned at her for a second, then nodded tersely. All three men stepped out, and a lock clicked shut on the other side of the door.

Now what was she supposed to do?

She thought fast. Jagger, Laura and Nick

were stuck aboard the *Veronique,* too. And if she knew AbaCo procedures, a detailed security sweep of the entire ship was commencing right about now. *A diversion.* She'd bet Jagger and company needed a diversion. But what? She eyed Schmeckler's computer. She moved around the desk to check it. Ha. Not only was it powered up, but it was still signed into the ship's internal computer network. What could she do with a computer to mess up a ship?

She recalled an argument she'd overheard some months back between Schroder and another man about a hole in the company's shipboard security having to do with shipboard weight and balance systems. Schroder had wanted it fixed and the other man had said it was too obscure to worry about, since only a few senior ship's officers had access to it. And this computer was already signed in to the very system that Schroder had been upset about.

Perfect.

Now, what was it Schroder had said? The volumes of air and water in a ship's massive ballast tanks—the bladders of air or water used to balance a ship laterally and keep it from rolling over on its side—could be changed by anyone with access to the ship's onboard load planning system. He'd been concerned that someone might hit the wrong button and accidentally empty a ballast tank.

She had to hunt around a bit in the load planning system, but then she found it. An innocuous little button that said Enter Ballast Corrections. She set all of the starboard ballast tanks on the *Veronique* to fill with air and all of the port-side tanks to flood with water. She suspected some sort of warning would go off on the bridge, too, and they'd try to override the command. To that end, she quickly typed up a logic loop that would keep her manual ballast commands active in spite of any overrides attempted from the bridge. She sent the miniprogram to the *Veronique's* mainframe.

When she got back a message that her program had been successfully installed, she hit the activation button to empty and fill the ballast tanks.

How long it would take for anything to

happen—if anything happened at all—she had no idea. She checked her cell phone to verify that the line was still connected to Schroder's cell phone. It seemed to be. She stuffed it back in her pocket.

Diversion hopefully complete, she went to work on escaping from Schmeckler's office. She hunted around in his desk until she found a pair of scissors, and then went to work on the door's hinges. It took her several minutes and resorting to using a heavy-duty stapler as a hammer, but she finally managed to wedge the bolt out of the top hinge. She crouched and went to work on the lower hinge. The bolt burst free, and she pressed her ear to the door to listen for movement outside. Nothing.

She pried the door back enough to slip through the gap and stepped out into the hall. If she wasn't mistaken, the floor wasn't entirely level beneath her feet. She raced down the hall until she found a stairwell, and she ran down the stairs as fast as she could. A placard said she was on deck eleven. Nine decks to go to reach the one with the hatch to the pier.

By the time she got about halfway down the stairs, the tilt beneath her feet was becoming more noticeable. She heard sounds of shouting from somewhere overhead, but the voices didn't sound as though they were headed her way.

She burst out onto deck two, and straight ahead was the gangway and the shore beyond. She slowed to a fast walk and approached the sailor stationed at the door. It was the same guy as before, and he was frantic with worry.

"What 'n hell's going on?" he all but bellowed at her.

"I don't know. I was talking to Schmeckler and all hell broke loose. They said something about topside cargo shifting and overbalancing the ship. She's rolling on her side and they can't stop it. They told me to get the heck off the *Veronique* before she sinks."

The sailor exploded into a string of curses. Then he pulled himself together enough to say, "You better go now. The gangplank's getting unsafe."

She stepped up to the door and looked out.

Sure enough, the metal walkway, which had been nearly level when she boarded, was now tilting down at the dock at an alarmingly steep angle.

She paused in the door to face the sailor. "You'd better get up top. They need all hands up there if they're gonna save the ship."

The sailor's eyes widened in panic and he bolted for the stairs.

She turned and started down the ramp. She ended up having to half run down the thing to keep her balance, but then she spurted out onto the pier and solid ground. She ran for shore and didn't stop until she'd cleared the main ship-yard and was standing once more in the dark shadows of the visitors' parking lot beside their car.

She swore under her breath. She didn't have the car keys. And she didn't have a clue how to break into a car, let alone hot-wire one. She turned to look back at the ship. It was defi-nitely listing to port. It was probably no more than a ten-degree angle, but in a ship the size of the *Veronique,* ten degrees made it look about ready to roll over and sink.

Sailors were running around on deck like furious fire ants, and she suspected some poor schmuck on the bridge was frantically trying to figure out why none of his commands to the ballast system were working. Personnel from the docks were starting to head toward the ship, and a number of them ran up the steep gangplank, no doubt trying to assist the disabled vessel.

Well, she'd created chaos. Now, if only Jagger, Laura and Nick could find a way off the ship in the midst of it all.

Chapter 16

Belowdecks, Jagger crouched and peeked around a corner. He'd taken point while Laura helped an exhausted Nick stumble along behind him. He was just in time to see the sailor on the watch bolt away from the main hatch into the bowels of the ship. He didn't know what the hell was going on with the *Veronique,* but it was definitely listing hard to port. Hey, he was all over any luck that came their way.

He signaled over his shoulder for the pair behind him to move out. Nick apparently knew military sign language, because he shambled forward immediately. The guy was obviously running on nothing but guts and grit, but so far, he'd clenched his jaw and managed to keep up.

Jagger approached the gangplank cautiously. Son of a gun. Not a soul was in sight. Were they actually going to be able to stroll off the ship? It seemed too easy to be true. But he was prepared to go with the easy solution right now. No telling how much longer Nick would be able to stay upright. The guy was as gray as a ghost.

Laura and Nick caught up to him and likewise gaped at the unattended hatch. "What's happening?" she whispered.

"I have no idea. But let's not stick around to find out. C'mon."

Jagger led the way, the butt of his sidearm tightly gripped in his fist inside the pocket of his jacket. This stunk of yet another AbaCo trap. But then, he'd successfully made it off the *Zhow Min* and he'd been sure that was a trap. Could lightning strike twice in one lifetime?

He headed down to the dock, looked both ways and waved Laura and Nick down. There was a tricky moment when Nick lost his balance, but Laura lunged forward and got a shoulder under the guy's armpit before he could go down.

Once they were safely on the pier, Jagger moved to Nick's other side and looped the taller man's arm over his shoulder. Between Jagger and Laura they all but carried him off the pier. And just in time, too. Behind them, a team of firefighters raced toward the *Veronique* and clambered aboard the wounded behemoth.

Jagger guided the awkward trio into the visitors' parking lot and his car. He looked around frantically. *Where is Emily?* Panic exploded behind his eyes, all but blinding him.

"Take the car and get Nick out of here, Laura. I'm going back for Em—"

An apparition rose from behind the car and he all but fainted in relief at the familiar shape of Emily coming around the rear fender. She flung herself at him with enough force to nearly knock him off his feet. She was sobbing so hard he couldn't make out a single word of whatever she cried against his chest.

"Easy, darlin'. We all made it. Let's get out of here. We'll talk later."

He opened the car door and eased her into the front passenger's seat. Nick had already half collapsed into the backseat, and Laura was climbing in beside him, cradling him close. Clearly those two had some sort of history between them. And given how badly steel-nerved Laura had fallen apart at the sight of the guy, it was an intimate emotional history.

Their departure was shockingly anticlimactic. He drove sedately out of the parking lot and pointed the car back toward the hills and valleys of the Shenandoah. The video camera was safely in his pocket, loaded with damning footage of Nick's prison and the container he'd been trapped within. Like him, Nick hadn't believed at first that rescue had arrived. He'd had to flash a few of his own scars to convince the guy that he, too, had been AbaCo's prisoner and was here to free the guy.

Jagger shuddered to remember the mental and emotional place he'd been in when Emily had done the same for him. He reached over and squeezed her hand.

"Okay, honey, it's safe to talk now. How did you get off the ship? And do you have any idea what happened to the *Veronique?*"

Emily ducked her head, abashed. "I broke into the ship's computer ballast system and filled all the starboard tanks with air and flooded all the port-side tanks. The computer indicated that the ship will only roll about eleven degrees before it stops."

Jagger gaped. And then he laughed, long and hard. He exulted. "Danger Girl rules!"

Emily's face went serious. Stubborn. "Danger Girl is dead. Your life is not for me. I can't do that again. I don't have the nerves for it, and I have a responsibility to my daughter. One parent who runs around risking life and limb for fun is enough for any child. I'm sorry, Jagger. I can't be part of your world."

He stared at her, stunned into silence. What was she saying? Was she dumping him? Was she tossing him out of her family's life? Not that he'd blame her. His world was far too dangerous for children to be around. Hell, hadn't his first thought when he found out Michelle existed been horror at what a horrendous liability she was to him?

Except those pink cheeks and bouncy golden curls and innocent laughter didn't feel like a liability. They felt like a little slice of heaven on earth. His own special angel come to save him from the dark.

"Em…" He didn't know what to say. He wanted to beg her to hang on to them, to allow him to be a part of their lives. But he didn't have any right at all to ask that of her. He clenched his jaw against the thickness in his throat and blinked hard against the burning in his eyes. Damned things had grit in them all of a sudden.

Nick passed out in the backseat. Hard to tell if he was sleeping or unconscious. Probably a little of both. Laura cradled the big man protectively in her arms and didn't look as though she planned on letting go for a very long time. Nick might actually get a happily ever after. Lucky bastard.

Emily stared out the window in pensive silence, her head turned away from Jagger. And he let her withdraw. It was possibly the hardest thing he'd ever done. But he let her go. What choice did he have? He loved her. Loved Michelle. Enough to leave them, to keep them safe from his world, to protect them from everything he did and was.

But it ripped his heart out of his chest and tore it to little shreds to do so.

They'd been driving for maybe a half hour when Emily murmured, frowning, "Schmeckler said something strange in his office...."

Jagger glanced over at her, his heart dead. "Who's Schmeckler?" he managed to choke out woodenly.

"The *Veronique's* security officer. He pulled me into his office and took away my ID badge. He was trying to call Schroder when a motion detector went off. I assume that was you guys."

Jagger nodded. "Probably. What did he say that's got you puzzled?"

"He was mad when the alarm went off. He mumbled something to himself in German about being undermanned tonight. And one of the guys with him mentioned a contingent of Schmeckler's men being ashore."

Wild alarms erupted in Jagger's gut. His every operative instinct, honed over twenty years, went onto high alert. He glanced in the rearview mirror, and Laura was staring back at him, horror written on her face.

Laura breathed, "It was too easy."

Jagger started to swear. He cursed long and hard as he stood on the accelerator and the car roared forward.

"What's wrong?" Emily cried. She might not be a trained spy, but she had good instincts, and she sensed that something was terribly wrong.

Jagger ground out, "Finding Nick's crate was too easy. The rescue went too smoothly, and we encountered practically no opposition."

"What are you saying?" she asked, with terrible certainty that she knew the answer to that vibrating in her voice.

He spelled it out. "Given that AbaCo knew they had a break-in to their special cargo database today, and they know you and I are in the local area, and they knew the *Veronique* was coming in today, does it make any sense at all that we all but strolled onto the ship, snagged Nick and strolled off again?"

Emily shook her head, her eyes the size of saucers.

"It was a diversion, Em. They drew us to the *Veronique* on purpose."

She frowned. "But they didn't catch us. Heck, they all but let me go."

"Exactly. That's because we weren't the target tonight."

"Then what was?"

"Not what," he said gently. "Who."

She stared for a moment more; then her face crumpled. "Oh, God. The children!"

Jagger closed his eyes for a moment as pain and terror slashed through him, but then focused on the road flying beneath their tires.

"What do you want to do, Jagger?" Laura asked grimly from the backseat.

He glanced over at Emily, who was a complete wreck, her fists stuffed against her mouth as if she'd scream if she moved them. "Make the call."

Laura nodded and held her cell phone to her ear. In a moment, she began to murmur unintelligibly.

Emily glanced back and forth between the two of them. "What's going on? Talk to me, Jagger!"

He sighed. "Laura's talking to the FBI. She'll ask them to send a large contingent of agents to her house. Which will protect the kids. But it will also ensure that I'm arrested."

"I'm wanted, too," she reminded him.

He nodded grimly. He knew what he had to do, but damn, it was hard. Harder even than he'd expected. He forced himself to continue speaking. "I'll drop you off outside her estate. Laura will make arrangements to reunite you with Michelle, and you two can leave the country. I've got some money squirreled away for emergencies, and you can have it. Laura will help you go someplace far, far away. Start a new life. Doris can go, too, if she wants."

"It's done," Laura announced from the backseat.

"Thanks," he replied. "I'll never be able to repay you for what you're doing for us."

Laura laughed without humor. "Are you kidding? You gave me the father of my son back."

Nick lurched beside her at that but didn't fully regain consciousness.

Emily's gaze went wild and she looked back and forth between Laura and Jagger. "No! I'm not leaving you!"

Each word was a dagger to his heart. "Honey, you have to. You said yourself that this life isn't for you. And it's not right for Michelle, either."

Emily subsided, sobbing into her sleeve. Each heave of her slender shoulders was agonizing to witness.

He reached across the car to touch her arm. "I'm so sorry, Em. So very sorry."

She shook off his hand. He let it fall.

How he stayed on the road for the next hour without wrapping the car around a tree, he had no idea. But eventually, Laura commenced calling out directions from the backseat. Apparently, there was a back entrance to the estate, and she guided him to it.

When they'd driven a ways into a stand of heavy woods and his direction sense said they were getting close to the house, he stopped the car.

"What're you doing?" Emily croaked.

"It's time, honey. You need to get out of the car, now. Laura will bring Michelle to you as soon as she can."

He climbed out of the car and went around to her side of the vehicle. He opened the door, but she merely stared up at him.

"Please, Emily. It's the only way."

"No, it's not."

His eyebrows lifted.

"I'm going with you. Don't make me choose between you and Michelle. I can't do it. You're the two halves of my heart, and I can't live without either one of you."

"But you'll be arrested, too—"

"I have faith in Laura's lawyers. They'll get me off. All I did was rescue you. And now that we've got that video, I'll be fine."

He shook his head in the negative. "I can't take that chance with you. I *have* to know the two of you will be safe—"

A faint rattling sound echoed through the trees and his head jerked up.

"Let's go, Jagger," Laura called urgently from the backseat. She'd recognized the sound, too. That was gunfire. Coming from the vicinity of the mansion. The mansion his precious daughter was currently inside.

Chapter 17

Emily's head jerked up. That sounded like…
ohmigod. "Was that a gunshot?"

"Several of them," Jagger bit out as he turned
and raced for the car's trunk.

Laura leaped out and joined him. The trunk
slammed shut, and Emily made out the thick,
tubular shapes of rifles. Several of them.

Jagger leaped into the driver's seat and rolled
the car forward in the dark.

Laura shook Nick awake. "Do you think you
can you shoot a rifle?"

He shrugged and answered in a rusty voice,
"I'm game to try."

Laura asked, "How 'bout if I tell you your
son, Adam, is inside that house down there

and AbaCo's thugs are trying to break into the place to kidnap him?"

Nick sat up straighter. "Oh, yeah. I can do this."

Emily lost it, then. "AbaCo's men are breaking in?" she squeaked.

Laura grinned. "They may get into the house, but there's no way they're getting into the safe room."

"The...what?" Emily turned around to face the other woman.

"The house has a safe room. I installed an old bank vault and equipped it with self-contained power generators, air filters, even a toilet and running water. I showed it to Doris before we left and gave her the combination to the door. I told her to spend the night in there with the kids just in case."

Now, if only Doris had taken Laura's suggestion to heart and taken precautions with the children.

Jagger stopped the car just inside the woods, maybe two hundred yards behind the house. "Can you see any movement?" he muttered.

Emily scanned the area around the house frantically but saw nothing. *Please, God, let this all be a giant false alarm.*

But then a flash of light from somewhere on the other side of the house lit up the night.

Jagger said, "Laura, you and Nick go in the family room doors. Emily and I will head in through the kitchen. Assuming we meet no opposition, we'll meet at the base of the stairs. AbaCo tends to use German ordnance and the FBI should come with bigger-caliber stuff."

The pair in the backseat nodded and slid out, weapons in hand, and disappeared into the dark.

"Where's my gun?" Emily demanded.

Jagger started. "Do you know how to use one?"

"Plenty well enough for tonight's purposes. My stepdad showed me how to handle a gun, but he never did talk me into going hunting with him. But if AbaCo guys are out there, I'm all over shooting them."

Jagger grinned and passed a shotgun across

to her. "C'mon, Mama Bear. Let's go protect your cub."

Grimly, she hefted the weapon and chambered a round. She stuffed the shells Jagger handed her into her pockets and then nodded her readiness. Michelle was in danger. She had to save her baby. Fear had no place in that equation and hovered only peripherally in the background of her mind.

Jagger's restraining hand on her arm was all that kept her from barging into the house, shotgun blazing. "Easy, Em. We don't know if the FBI's on scene yet. If you just charge in there, they may shoot you."

"The gunfire came from out front. I'm betting AbaCo's guys are in the house shooting out and the FBI is just arriving on scene."

"The FBI's not stupid. They will surround the house."

"But they haven't yet, or else we wouldn't have been able to run up to the back door like this."

Jagger nodded. "Good point. So let's go find

those AbaCo bastards and wreck their evening."

She nodded her approval at that plan and realized her entire body was shaking. Okay, so she was actually terrified somewhere deep in her gut. But it wasn't as though she had any choice in what she was about to do. Michelle needed her. End of discussion.

Jagger whispered one last set of instructions. "Stay behind me. Your job is to make sure no one sneaks up on us from behind. I'll take care of engaging with the bad guys. Keep your head down and don't be a hero, got it?"

"Got it."

Jagger eased open the kitchen door and, crouching in the dark, made his way behind the big center island. Emily followed close behind. As they paused, silence settled around them for a moment. But then, the noises of movement came from toward the front of the house. Whoever was already in the mansion was making no attempt at stealth.

Jagger raised a hand and started to wave her forward, but his hand froze in midair as a loud voice shouted through a megaphone from out front, "FBI! Lay down your weapons and come out with your hands clasped behind your necks."

Thank God.

Profound relief washed over Emily that help was here. But as she exhaled in gratitude, another sound caused her to stiffen once more. A voice, speaking in terse German. Giving orders.

She leaned forward and whispered frantically in Jagger's ear, "He just ordered his men to abandon the mission. They're to fall back to the kitchen and run for the woods and meet at some rendezvous point. They're coming right at us!"

Jagger nodded and settled his weapon more securely in his arms. Without him having to say anything, she did the same, fitting the butt of the shotgun firmly against her shoulder.

Running footsteps pounded down the hall. The swinging kitchen door burst open and Jagger shouted in credible German, "Freeze!"

The AbaCo men—six of them—lurched

violently to a halt, their weapons trained on the kitchen island. One of them snarled, "Lay down your weapons and get out of our way or we will shoot you both."

Ohgodohgodohgod...

Michelle. She must hold her ground for her baby. For the man in front of her. For her family.

Jagger snapped back, "Not happening, you Stasi SOB. It's over. You're busted."

The German grinned. "I think not. You're not FBI. Kill them—"

His command was cut off by the sound of at least a dozen weapons clicking to the ready behind Emily. A new voice spoke calmly. "Nope, they're not FBI, but we are."

Emily all but fainted, she was so light-headed with relief.

"Everybody, lay down your weapons slowly."

Emily complied along with Jagger and the German hit squad before them. As the Germans were straightening back up, one of them reached out fast and flipped on the kitchen lights. He dived for his weapon...

…and was dead before he hit the floor.

The other Germans froze in various bent and crouched postures in the act of reaching for their weapons.

Four FBI agents wearing black Windbreakers raced into the room, flanking the island. Another half dozen came in through the door, spreading out behind Emily and Jagger. From her prone position on the floor, they were just about the prettiest sight she'd seen since Jagger had looked up at her inside his crate.

"Glad you could make it, gentlemen," Jagger commented from beside her.

"You Jagger Holtz?" someone asked from behind them.

"That's me. Two more good guys are moving in the other end of the house—a woman and a tall, skinny guy with a beard."

"Thanks for the invite to this little party. We're looking forward to talking to you and the woman. That her with you?"

"Yup."

"Stay put on the floor while we secure these bastards. We'll get back to you in a minute."

Emily complied, watching as the FBI team handcuffed and searched the Germans. An arsenal of weapons and gear grew beside the Germans. It took several minutes, but finally the FBI men hauled the AbaCo team to its feet and marched them outside.

One of the FBI men approached Jagger and Emily. "I'm gonna have to search you both. Standard procedure after a firefight. Then you can get up."

It wasn't that bad, actually. The guy was fast and impersonal and she fixed an image of Michelle in her mind.

As soon as she was upright, she asked, "Where's my daughter?"

"We haven't found any children in the house, ma'am. But the safe room's locked down. We're guessing the kids are in there."

Just then, Laura and Nick were escorted into the kitchen. Laura asked the agent talking to them, "Could someone get some orange juice out of the refrigerator for my friend here? He's on the verge of passing out."

Nick did, indeed, look like death warmed

over in the room's bright lights. Laura explained quickly that he'd also been imprisoned on an AbaCo ship, as Jagger had, and furthermore, they had video of his rescue to prove it. The FBI men looked extremely interested, and if Emily wasn't mistaken, the government agents' postures relaxed even more toward her and Jagger.

Hope turned into certainty that she and Jagger were going to be okay. They'd gotten the evidence they needed to prove their innocence. Between the four of them, Laura, Nick, Jagger and she should be able to bury AbaCo so deep it never came up for air again.

An agent poured Nick a glass of juice, which he sipped in unadulterated bliss. Jagger made a commiserating sound from beside her and muttered under his breath, "Wait till he gets his first chocolate. The guy'll think he died and went to heaven."

She murmured back, "Gee, I thought heaven was that night on Lyle's beach."

"You have no idea. Believe me. I *knew* I'd died and gone to heaven then."

Laura spoke from across the room. "Can I go open the vault now? Nick wants to meet his son, and I expect Emily and Jagger want to hug their daughter."

"Now, there's an understatement," Emily declared.

Jagger looped his arm around her shoulders and smiled down at her. "Let's go get our daughter. And remind me to thank Doris every day for the rest of her life for protecting the kids."

A team of FBI agents trailed along as the party made its way to the front stairs. Laura opened a paneled door and a steel, bank-vault-style door loomed. Emily waited impatiently as Laura entered a lengthy code into an electronic keypad, then grabbed the heavy crossbar and gave a tug. The door cracked open.

"Doris, it's Laura and Emily and Jagger. We're out here with a bunch of FBI agents. It's okay to come out now."

A light went on just inside the vault as several FBI agents pulled the massive door all the way open. Adam ran out first, straight into his mother's arms. Nick stared in awe at his son as though he'd never get enough of the sight of the child. Laura glanced up at him worriedly, and then smiled brilliantly.

"Now that you're home, I guess my days as MysteryMom are over."

Emily gaped as Doris exclaimed, "You're Mystery Mom?"

Laura grinned and explained, "I've been searching for Nick ever since he first disappeared five years ago. To keep from going crazy while I hunted for him, I started helping other moms find fathers for their children. Their successes kept my own hope alive for one day finding Adam's father."

Emily blurted, "You sent me that e-mail about Jagger?"

"I didn't know it was Jagger, but I'd figured out that AbaCo might be keeping prisoners on ships in international waters. That one container never got off-loaded and always had a weight that didn't match up with its reported cargo."

"How did you know to send that e-mail to me, then?" Emily asked.

Doris cleared her throat. "That would be my fault. I contacted MysteryMom to ask her if she could help find Michelle's father."

Emily stared. She'd had no idea her mom had done that.

Laura continued, "I hadn't made any progress at finding Jagger, but I found out you worked at AbaCo and started poking around there. That's when I spotted the suspicious containers and started tracking them. By the way, in that printout of special cargo you ran for us yesterday, I've spotted a half dozen more suspicious containers."

One of the FBI men commented, "We'll be happy to look into those. I expect we'll be looking into a whole lot of AbaCo's activities real soon."

Jagger's arm tightened about Emily's shoulders. "So I guess I also owe my rescue to you, Laura, and to my future mother-in-law, too."

"Your future—" Emily's gaze snapped up to his. "What are you saying, Jagger?"

"I'm saying that I want to marry you. What do you say, Em?"

Joy exploded behind her eyeballs until everything was so bright she could barely look at him. The FBI men around them grinned. But then reality came crashing back in on her so hard she could hardly breathe. It felt as if an anvil had just landed on her chest.

"You know I love you, Jagger."

"I love you, too."

Whoa. She almost lost her train of thought at hearing those words from him. She wanted to beg him to say it again. To mean it enough to change for her. But then he wouldn't be the man she loved anymore.

She blurted, "But I'm not Danger Girl."

Jagger blinked down at her, clearly confused.

"Ever since that night we met, I've been trying to be the kind of woman James Bond could fall in love with. But—" she took a deep breath and forced herself onward in a rush "—it's not me. I can't live a life of danger and excitement. I'm a homebody. I like safety. Peace and quiet. I'll never be glamorous or wild or dangerous. I want to stay home and raise Michelle and live a boring, normal life. I'm just me."

Jagger listened intently to her outburst, but by the end of it, a tiny smile was starting to play at the corners of his mouth.

"What?" she demanded. Here she'd just laid out her guts for him. Explained why she couldn't marry him no matter how much she loved him, and he thought it was funny?

"Honey, I'm not James Bond. I'm not some Super Spy, either."

"Yeah, but you love this life. You love running around in the dark with guns and rescuing people. It's who you are."

"I hate to disappoint you, but my twenty-year mark in the military passed while I was cooped up in that container. I'm eligible to retire, and I have every intention of doing so as soon as I can fill out the paperwork."

"But what about tonight? Nick's rescue..." she sputtered.

"I told you I couldn't in good conscience walk away from another prisoner in a box and not try to help the guy. And yeah, I wanted to get enough evidence to sink AbaCo. But I'm done living on the wild side. Super Spy has hung up his cloak and called it quits. Within about thirty seconds of seeing you and Michelle together for the first time, I knew I wanted nothing more than to spend the rest of my nice, boring life with you two."

"Really?" she asked in a small voice. Hope hovered at the edges of her heart, but she wasn't quite ready to let it in.

"I want to watch Michelle grow up. I want to terrorize her boyfriends and give her a couple of brothers or sisters. I want to sit on my front porch in a rocking chair and watch the sun set. And I want to wake up every morning for the rest of my life and watch the sunrise in your eyes."

Tears she didn't even know were there spilled over onto her cheeks.

Jagger looked alarmed. "Hey. Are you okay, honey?"

"I'm more than okay. I'm perfect. Everything's *perfect*."

"Help me out here, Em. Does that mean you'll marry me?"

"Yes. Oh, yes!"

He wrapped his arms around both of them and squeezed until Michelle squawked, "Jaggy too tight!"

Laughing, Emily looked down at their daughter. "This is your daddy, Michelle. Can you say daddy?"

"Da-da."

Joy broke across Jagger's face that shot all the way to the bottom of her heart.

"Dadadadadadada!" Michelle squealed.

Danger Girl and the Super Spy might not live beyond this night's work, but it didn't matter. They had the strongest bond of all to protect them and keep them safe against life's struggles. A family.

Their family.

* * * * *